Praise for *Don't Tell Mum I Work on the Rigs, She Thinks I'm a Piano Player in a Whorehouse*

'Not so much a thriller as a driller, *Don't Tell Mum* is our tip for Bloke's Book of the Year (BBOTY).'

Sunday Telegraph

'. . . a humorous, politically incorrect boy's own adventure . . . blokey bonding, brawls and bravado . . .'

The Daily Telegraph

'A torrent of tall tales from a life less ordinary.'

The Press and Journal, Aberdeen

'A fascinating and funny life story well worth the read.'

Sportsladsmag.com

'The mass appeal is obvious. Full of colourful stories and well-worn anecdotes accumulated over almost two decades working on the oil rigs.'

TNT Magazine

'Carter's tales are always entertaining and offer a few unblinking aperçus about Big Oil seen from the inside.'

Scotland on Sunday

'Ever wondered what happens to the boys from the movie *Jackass* when they grow up? They become oil rig workers. Shit happens, so some of the stuff that Paul Carter and his friends get hit with probably isn't their fault—although sitting at the top of an oil rig derrick during a thunderstorm is probably inviting God to hit you with something. Otherwise most of the madness and mayhem, interspersed with the occasional car or motorcycle accident and totally over the top practical jokes, are clearly all down to Paul. As for the chain-smoking monkeys, pool-playing ferrets and bartending orangutans . . . if the humans are crazy the animals should be too.'

Tony Wheeler, founder of Lonely Planet

'. . . a Boy's Own yarn from the front line of the oil industry.'

Men's Style

'. . . literary black gold . . . horrifying and hilarious.'

Sun Herald

'This is one of the most split-my-sides-laughing memoirs I think I have ever read . . . that blows along like the North Sea.'

Northern Star

'What you have here . . . is that rare situation of somebody who not only has a story to tell but the ability to tell it. Carter's anecdotes are told with great humour and perfect timing.'

The Age

'This . . . is not for the fainthearted . . . For less sensitive readers, there is a lot of fun to be had from Carter's *Don't Tell Mum I Work on the Rigs* . . . With his earthy language and character sketches, Carter makes a basic autobiography into one wild ride, leaving you wondering how this guy isn't dead.'

Entrophy

'This is one of those fantastic read-'em-in-a-day books that has you attached like Velcro from the first paragraph . . . It's not literature, but it's not boring . . . A boy's own romp around the globe, *Don't Tell Mum* is perfect for lovers of high adventure/mongrel humour and would attract even the most resistant male readers. It's *Auf Wiedersehen, Pet* crossed with Barry Crump on speed and I loved it.'

Wanganui Chronicle

'This is a book for blokes . . . Carter is a kind of modern day Indiana Jones . . . a natural storyteller.'

Sunday Tasmanian

'. . . a laconic larrikin, with a tale that is full of humour . . . A refreshing memoir, Paul Carter is a genuine Australian character.'

Manly Daily

THIS IS NOT A DRILL

THIS IS NOT A DRILL

JUST ANOTHER GLORIOUS DAY IN THE OILFIELD

PAUL CARTER

NICHOLAS BREALEY PUBLISHING

LONDON • BOSTON

First published in the UK by
Nicholas Brealey Publishing in 2007

3–5 Spafield Street
Clerkenwell, London
EC1R 4QB, UK
Tel: +44 (0)20 7239 0360
Fax: +44 (0)20 7239 0370

20 Park Plaza, Suite 1115A
Boston
MA 02116, USA
Tel: (888) BREALEY
Fax: (617) 523 3708

www.nicholasbrealey.com
www.paulcarter.net.au

ISBN-13: 978-1-85788-500-2
ISBN-10: 1-85788-500-7

British Library Cataloguing in Publication Data
A catalogue record for this book is available from the British Library.

Front cover photo: Ian Holland, Big Stock Photo
Author photo on back cover: Stephen Oxenbury Photography

Printed in the UK by Clays Ltd, St Ives plc.

CONTENTS

And the sea will grant each man new hope,
As sleep brings dreams of home.

Christopher Columbus

IMMIGRATION AUSTRALIA
19 AUG 2005
DEPARTED
AUSTRALIA
SYDNEY AIRPORT 3480
Type/Type
Surname/Nom (1)
CARTER
Given names/Prénoms (2)
PAUL ALEXANDER
Nationality/Nationalité (3)
BRITISH CITIZEN
Date of birth/Date de naissance (4)
Sex/Sexe (5)
Place of birth/Lieu de naissance (6)
Date of issue/Date de délivrance (7)
Authority/Autorité (8)
Date of expiry/Date d'expiration (9)
Holder's signature/Signature
UNITED KINGDOM
Passport No.
Name of bearer
Nom du titulaire
Accompanied by spouse
Accompagné de son épouse
National status
Nationalité
15 FEB 2006
PERMITTED TO ENTER AND REMAIN IN SINGAPORE FOR THIRTY DAYS FOR SOCIAL VISIT ONLY FROM DATE SHOWN ABOVE.
ARTER<<PAUL<ALXX
IMMIGRATION
21 AUG 2005
815 SINGAPORE 815
VISIT PASS
Subject to Reg. 12 (7)
Immigration Regulations
19 AUG 2005
PERMITTED TO ENTER AND REMAIN IN SINGAPORE FOR THIRTY DAYS FOR SOCIAL VISIT ONLY FROM DATE SHOWN ABOVE.

1 SILENT ALARM

'Just another glorious day in the oilfield,' said Erwin.

I could only look at him. I had stopped feeling my feet ten minutes ago; my hands were so cold that I wasn't sure they would stay whole if I tried to move them.

In front of me was an assortment of 120 men in various stages of undress, all moving in super-fast time, all with the same strained, panic-stricken expression on their face. The sort of face you pull when the hotel door slams shut just as you are putting the room service tray out in the hall and you realise you're locked out and naked. Except this was no hotel corridor, this was a semi-submersible drilling rig . . . in imminent danger of becoming a submersible-we're-all-fucked-and-half-of-us-can't-swim rig.

It's 2 a.m., minus thirty-six degrees celsius, we're miles from land and the rig is capsizing. In the middle of the insanity and chaos stood Erwin, that familiar lazy grin seesawing across his face.

The abandon-rig alarm went off some ten minutes ago. 'THIS IS NOT A DRILL' is all I remember hearing. As soon as I got out of bed I knew it was serious. The rig was listing five degrees to port. We've got fifteen minutes to get to our lifeboat. The fluorescent lights blinked on. 'This is not a drill.' Again the recorded voice. The continous ringing of the alarm made a fist in my gut. As I scrambled to rip my survival suit out of its bag I could feel the rig slowly continue to tip. This is really happening, I thought, this is not a drill.

The abandon-rig alarm is the one sound you never ever want to hear on an offshore drilling rig, especially when the water temperature kills after just three minutes. Its sound bores right through you, getting through to your brain faster than anything you could imagine. It's all the motive you need to get to a lifeboat no matter what gets in your way. It's a licence to survive with an international adaptor on it, everyone instantly knows the score and it sorts out the men from the boys quicker than anything I've seen. Adrenaline burned in my joints. In fifteen years, this was my first abandon-rig alarm.

My survival immersion suit, I must have it ready, get out, get out now.

Dave, my room-mate, tore open his locker and started throwing stuff all over the place. I opened the door and shot a glance down the corridor; rubbish was scattered everywhere, in every room gear was flying out the door. What is it about abandoning a rig and the threat of dying through the most excruciating freezing process imaginable that brings out the litterbug in people? Men ran in all directions. Some, ripped from their sleep, stood dumbfounded in their jocks, unable to focus. No-one yelled or tried to communicate, everyone was concentrating on getting to their lifeboat in time with the right gear.

Slow down, get it right, I screamed silently and forced myself to check. Survival suit on, seals intact, life jacket on, passport, wallet. I went for the door.

'Smokes!' yelled Dave. 'You'll need them.' He was shoving a whole carton of Camels down the front of his survival suit.

We exploded out of our room and sprinted down the corridor. Red lights flashed, the alarm had turned into a hum . . . I had blanked it out, wasn't listening now. How much time have I wasted? Are we at eight or nine degrees now?

Both of us were only too aware that if the listing got

to ten degrees then they couldn't launch the lifeboats. We passed the galley, unwittingly smashing plates and glasses that littered the floor. A young kitchenhand stood in the middle of the debris, wearing only the bottom half of his thermal underwear, his bare feet bleeding onto the floor and a yellow streak running down his right leg. Dave went straight through him. If this guy couldn't get himself to his lifeboat, we weren't going to stop and give him directions.

We took the stairs three at a time. Lifeboat number 1 was on the starboard side, right under the heli-deck, but it may as well have been in Cleveland. Something inside the room we needed to cross had slid across the floor and blocked our escape; the door was stuck.

'OUTER STAIRWELL, GO GO!' I turned around and ran back the way we had come, precious minutes wasted. There was real fear in Dave's voice, it made me move faster.

We went back through the galley, the kitchenhand had disappeared. At the far end of the corridor was a hatch to the outer stairwell; I hit it so hard I felt my shoulder crack as it flew open. We descended the stairs without really touching them. The freezing air bit into the sweat on my face, and everything lay at a bizarre angle as the rig slowly continued to tip. Dave lost his footing at the bottom of the stairs and went down hard into a container that lay across the walkway. We were fifty yards from our secondary lifeboat. I pulled him up and turned to run. The crew were mustering and preparing to launch what looked more like an orange submarine than a boat. Someone was there in the flashing light. It was Erwin, standing on the ramp in front of the open hatch. 'COME ON, RUN AS FAST AS YOU FUCKING CAN!' He was pulling us forward with his mind and giant hand gestures.

Dave passed me like an orange Carl Lewis and boarded in standard 'I'm not going to die out here' fashion, diving into the open hatch head first, having just ran a quarter mile of corridors in record time wearing a survival suit. I was happy he went through the hatch first as he cushioned my fall. My shoulder, his badly sprained ankle and our respective head injuries didn't stop the wonderful sense of elation that swept over us as Erwin slammed the hatch door and locked it down.

Andy the skipper was, as he liked to put it, 'well hard', and took every opportunity to give me his opinion on my new work boots. My feet were sticking straight up in front of him as I had landed upside down between two seats. 'They're so gay,' he said and grinned, pointing at my boots, on his way to the pilot's seat.

His left hand started the deluge pump then opened the air system, pressurising the vessel, while his right primed and started the motor in well-rehearsed synchronicity. We all sat there strapped into four-point harnesses, collectively focused on Andy's left hand hovering over the launch handle.

Dave pulled out the carton of Camels and passed it around. One by one each man nervously did that self pat-down thing you do when you need a light. Dave looked around at forty guys, each with a cigarette hanging from their bottom lip, looking blankly back. 'Not one of you dickheads brought a lighter, did you?'

Andy had an emergency radio pressed to his ear, waiting for the word. 'Stand by' was all we heard. Another ten minutes, a lifetime. 'Okay guys, it's a ballast control fuck-up. We have to wait,' he said. I strapped myself into a seat.

An hour went slowly by, my bum was going numb. Finally Andy put down the radio. 'It's under control. They lost a valve and the port-side pontoon started filling up with sea water, and then the emergency pump failed to start,' he explained. 'So now they have re-ballasted down on the starboard side to level out the rig while they try to fix the valve and pump. We have to wait in case they can't do it and we sink.'

'I'm glad I'm not the poor bastard trying to fix that pump,' said Dave.

Another hour and the situation was under control.

It took just fifteen minutes to get 120 men into the right gear and in a lifeboat. Not bad. The door that Dave and I couldn't open was blocked by a desk that slid across the room at just the right angle to stop us from getting it open. My shoulder was okay, but it was going to hurt for a couple of weeks. Dave got a nail gun from the warehouse and the desk was soon permanently fastened to the floor.

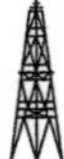

My first encounter with the oil world was early on in my life.

I was around ten when my mother started working at Tri-State Oil Tools; it was during the boom years in the early eighties when increasingly more offshore activity was turning Aberdeen, where we lived at the time, into the new centre of the oil industry in Europe. It had the largest heliport in Britain, ferrying men from all over the world offshore. The workshop next to my mother's office pulled at me like a giant magnet. There was a perpetual stream of oil men passing through and every last one of them had a story or a dirty joke to tell. I started skipping school to hang around and listen to them on crew change, swapping stories and talking shop. They gave me the odd glass of beer, shoved American money in my pockets, gave me knives, ball caps and dirty magazines. I loved them.

It didn't take long really. As soon as I was old enough I started roughnecking on a land rig and that was it.

The oilfield is a strange beast. It can quite unexpectedly creep under your skin and become as compulsive as your favourite legal addictive stimulant. I was hooked, and I still am. Although now the characters I wanted to be as a boy are getting harder to find. You have to really look for them as our brave new oilfield embraces shiny new Health, Safety and Environmental policies, Preventative Maintenance is of course paramount, and don't even think about stepping out on deck unless you can identify at least half a dozen hazards to correct. All this does help save lives and avoid accidents. Whole fleets of brand new sixth generation, fly by wire cyber rigs are getting spat out of shipyards all over the world at the moment, with new improved crews.

The guys at the top—the big players and the politicians they grease—will go on exploiting natural resources for generations. The rigs will still be drilling long after our current power brokers are gone and the next wave of bureaucrats have grown up ripping off a few Third World nations, backslapped their way into a massive retirement package and wobbled their massive bottoms up and down some Iberian beach playing crazy golf until they drop dead, unloved, in their mock Tudor retirement McMansions.

The guys at the coalface I looked up to are still

around, mind you, but not for much longer. They're all hitting their sixties, leaving the rigs and taking with them that wonderful old-school oilfield headspace. The one I listened to so carefully as a boy. But still, I find myself in the oilfield . . .

The Russian rig was always going to be fun. It was real frontier bullshit, with genuine old-school oilfield bad boys and guys who are so far gone all they know is drilling and that's it. They don't give a shit about anything but the rig and God help anyone who can't fit in.

I was thankful Erwin was there. He's our most senior offshore operator, a big man with broad shoulders and a hard, level gaze. Now in his mid-fifties, he is the most experienced and easily the best operator I have seen. Erwin has done it all; run every kind of pipe, on every kind of rig, on three continents, in more than a dozen countries. The first time I went offshore, wet behind the ears and totally ignorant of rig life, I met Erwin and instantly liked him. A few years later, after rig-hopping around South-east Asia, I landed a spot on his crew. I was lucky—his reputation is well-deserved, though he never brags about it. He taught me with a combination of patience and good humour, and guided me through my first five years in the oilfield.

Without trying, Erwin always retains a presence of authority and calm even when the worst is happening all around him. He's the guy with the light around him, the one that looks like he's got a weapons-grade temper but in fact doesn't.

Erwin's presence instantly lifted my mood, and within a few days of his arrival we were all joking and laughing about the operation. You know, 'Gee whiz, we all nearly drowned yesterday', that kind of thing.

My crew on this gig were all from Azerbaijan and finished every sentence with 'fargin'. They'd walk up to me and say, 'Paul, when we go to town drink vodka fargin?', 'I don't like Russia rig . . . food no good fargin'. And so on.

On the rig, I was sharing a room with three blokes: 'Sick Boy', who didn't talk much and snored like a pit bull being hot-waxed; a very nice Canadian named Dave Nordli who everyone called 'The Seal Basher'; and a habitual alcoholic called 'Vodka Bob', who had the DTs—the shakes—so bad he couldn't fill out his daily report.

Vodka Bob drinks Guinness for breakfast when he's not on the rig. Sometimes he chases it with Smirnoff neat. His prefabricated concrete flat is cheaply furnished and sits in a run-down housing estate in Moscow, but it's better stocked with liquor than your average supermarket. He's been working offshore for fifteen years—the same as me, only Bob has not been as lucky.

Bob got up around six. I watched his ritual every morning. As he took long drags on a Texas Five, he'd put on his gear, slipping his fingers into leather gloves creased and moulded from the cast of his hard, thick hands. He's thirty-six, the same age as me, his body strong—not toned like you see reflected in overpriced gym mirrors in Sydney, but powerful from years of heavy work. It's work that's kept Bob alive, because if it were not for his regular abstinence enforced by the no-alcohol rule offshore, Bob would have drank himself to death years ago. Vodka Bob performed this routine each morning in meditative silence, under the watchful eyes of 1998's Playmate of the Month, who was taped to the wall by the shelf above his bunk. She was vaguely reflected in the tattoo descending Vodka Bob's back. He'd pull a comb through his long hair and have a last drag on his smoke. He was ready for work.

I think Bob had a better sense of himself by the end of his hitch offshore, his body winning a war of attrition against his will to drink. If only he could find the strength to avoid the bottles lining his flat.

Sick Boy was one of the assistant drillers. He's big, covered in tattoos, lives in Thailand and roars around the rig with a broad Scottish accent and a never-ending ability to make you laugh. He was fun to be around, and the drill floor was always organised when Sick Boy and the other AD, Scott, were around. Sick Boy got his name for all sorts of reasons. Besides knowing how to bleed and butcher a human, he is a skilled storyteller and exponent of the cling-wrapped toilet bowl. If it's done right, you just don't see the plastic stretched across the bowl until you stand up and wonder why your poo is levitating.

Kamran was one of my guys. He's a monster really, six foot eight inches tall, three hundred pounds, with a neck the same circumference as my thigh. His hands are so big I can't shake them properly. And he's a true walking penis; all he talks about is chasing women. I think he's been on the rig for far too long; he should be sent home next week.

The Americans on board got on very well with the Russians, there was a sense of mutual respect that hovered around their interactions. And modern Russia was alive and well, you could tell from all the vodka that somehow found its way on board one day. Its presence instantly lifted our comrades' moods, smoothed out any dramas and turned them into toilet humour, in a Boris Yeltsin kind of way.

Most of the American guys on the rig were from Louisiana; they're all Coonasses (Cajuns), you know. Considering they had just lost twenty-two rigs in one hit and most of New Orleans to Hurricane Katrina, they were in relatively good spirits. It was us guys out there manning dodgy rigs in the Russian sea who were taking a chance. The seas there are notoriously wild. The choppers were older than me and could only fly by line of sight; they regularly had to turn back because of the weather. That got interesting when they were past their PNR (point of no return). With half their fuel gone, they were committed to finding the rig in fog thicker than a 'Big Brother' housemate. So if anyone was going to get hurt, it was meant to be us. Not the boys drilling a couple of miles offshore from Bourbon Street.

Only a few days after the abandon-rig alarm, the weather turned nasty. We had a fire and H_2S drill on the same morning, with wild seas, a listing rig and the wind blowing at sixty-five knots. Hard-hats were flying all over the place and the drill was a complete shambles. The tool pusher—the rig name for the drilling manager—was so angry he wanted to keep doing the drill until we got it right, but the weather was too bad to do it safely. He wouldn't give the muster list and radio to the company man so he could shut it down, and I eventually had to talk the radio out of his hand; he was like a retired greyhound with a stuffed rabbit. There was a massive hurricane tracking up towards us and all reports suggested it was bad. We were thinking we might have to evacuate to the 'Asylum', a former Soviet mental institution that now houses offshore personnel en route to the rig and the closest thing to a hotel for hundreds of miles. I'd stayed there before. It was creepy and still a dump, but with vodka now . . . super.

The H_2S is a bastard drill to do in bad weather, but you've got to do it. It's called a 'sour well' when we encounter H_2S, or hydrogen sulphide gas. H_2S can hide in the formation and slowly migrate to the surface; it's heavier than air, completely odourless and deadly. Just one hundred parts per million will kill a man in a few seconds. It's very similar to potassium sulphide, the gas once used to put criminals to death in America's judicial gas chambers.

The worst case of H_2S happened a few years ago on an offshore rig. Everyone except the derrickman was killed. He was working at the top of the derrick and was therefore well above the deadly invisible cloud that engulfed the rig. All he could do was watch as one after another the crew just dropped to their death.

With no warning because the gas has no smell, you don't even know that you've breathed it in, you just suddenly asphyxiate. On a brighter note, we have gas detectors that go off like a howitzer if someone so much as farts, so no-one was going to drop dead on my watch!

There was a Spanish 'mud logger' on the rig called Miguel. Miguel made the drilling fluid we pump down the well. He spent his days in the mud pits, basically a big dark steamy room located deep in the bowels of the rig with huge vats of thick, slimy drilling mud. He wore what looked like a badly made 1960s sci-fi spacesuit, which in turn made him walk like the monster from *Young Frankenstein* and sound like a Spanish Darth Vader. He had to wear it because he was mixing the kind of nasty chemicals that would rot your head off, disfigure the next five generations of your offspring and make you internally combust if you got too close. It's a lonely job but Miguel seemed to enjoy it. I think on some level the suit gave him power, like when grown men think, just for a second, that their power drill is actually a machine gun.

When we were out here last year Miguel was very upset that we didn't have any movies to watch. 'Dis eez fakin sheet,' he protested, his accent so thick he would have a UN interpreter squinting in desperate concentration. But this year Miguel came prepared with more than two hundred DVDs, and was soon the most popular mud logger in history. For a while there everyone was banging on his cabin door twenty-four hours a day as they all have laptops and very short attention spans.

After a couple of days Miguel got pissed off with this and said he would ration the movies to one per day, of his choosing, to be screened at 7 p.m. So one night all the guys on day shift settled down in the big TV room to wait for Miguel. He walked in, striding confidently down the centre aisle. 'I hab a super mobie por cho guys,' he said, smiling. When Miguel smiled, you smiled back, not out of politeness, but because he's so scary. Apart from being a big man, Miguel has a face that looks like it's been set on fire a couple of times and put out with a cricket bat.

Miguel held out the disc in his big, weird hand—years of chemical burns had turned it into leather from a mad cow—pressed the open button on the player and dropped the disc into its cradle. Little lights flickered to life on the display. Miguel turned back to face the packed TV room and proudly announced, 'Di Cunt of Monte Christo.'

After that, he didn't share with anyone. People were paging him on the rig's PA system, 'Can the Cunt of Monte Christo pick up line one please?' The 'Monte Christo mud pits', as the sign read, was not a place to venture alone, as the 'Cunt' himself was a force to be feared and in that spacesuit he cut a fearsome profile.

I went down one day and found Miguel skulking about with a sack of caustic soda that weighs more than I do casually balanced over his huge right arm. 'Hi Miguel,' I said, looking him directly in the eye—literally, as he only has one—and smiled. 'Brought you a coffee, mate.' I handed the mug over. He knew we were shut down waiting for a chopper to arrive. Work has to stop for half an hour as the crane cannot operate if a helicopter is on final approach. We sat down on some big sacks of Christ-knows-what and had a good bullshit; he was laughing by the time I pulled on my gloves and stepped out through the hatch.

Later that afternoon Miguel brushed past me in the hall and shoved something in my top pocket. I looked down, a little confused, and pulled out a Vequeros Colorado Maduro cigar. These are easily one of the best Cuban cigars, but also one of the hardest to find because they don't have propylene glycol in them, an additive used in the humidification process. Without it, export outside Cuba is 'impossible' unless you happen to find yourself in a Russian mud pit talking to a Spanish one-eyed mud logger.

I'm not kidding about Miguel's eye—he got some acid in it years ago on some God-awful rig in Brazil and lost it. His favourite party trick is to pop out his false eye and quietly drop it in your beer. Then just as you're finishing off your pint you pull focus on an eyeball rolling through the foam towards your open mouth. Without his prosthetic eye, which at best resembles an old marble because of too many drunken episodes that ended with it rolling about on some bar room floor, Miguel looks like he should be put down—or perhaps just left in his spacesuit to creep around in the mud pits.

Miguel rides a Harley Dyna Wide Glide and is a card-carrying member of the 'Sons of Bitches', a motorcycle club of which Erwin and I are also members, although by law in his country you can't ride a bike with only one eye. Miguel dropped it a few years back when some housewife pulled out in front of his bike on a suburban road. The impact was minimal but contained just enough force to pop out his eye. He picked himself up to confront a tearful middle-aged lady, who fainted when Miguel casually retrieved the eye that was rattling about in his helmet and stuck it back in his head.

Weeks slowly rolled by as temperatures plummeted. The weather regularly pummelled us with blizzards, and on the drill floor the work was hard. The rig was not winterised; there was very little protection from the constant wind and snow. Every few hours the rig's vibration would shake free giant clumps of ice from the cross members of the derrick above us, sending frozen missiles down to shatter on the cold steel floor. Choppers were few and far between, and guys started to miss their crew-change dates, unable to get off the rig. Even the supply boats could not get in for days on end. It all took its toll on the crew, and eventually we started to run out of food, with the offerings up in the galley starting to look less like a decent meal and more like something you'd throw in the dog's bowl. Tempers frayed. I tried to keep my boys in good humour, but sometimes jokes aren't enough, and sometimes morale degenerates to the point where a fight kicks off. Usually explosive and short, fights on a rig tend to be vicious as no-one is prepared to back down, so they fight harder. The resulting 'What happened?' questions are almost unanimously answered in the same way, with the standard 'He fell'. Or the most popular and timeless 'I walked into a door'.

It happened so much that the company put up signs in a vain attempt to stop the boys from scrapping—or maybe it was to encourage a more creative line of excuses. It was a little hard to believe that anyone could reasonably walk into a door on the rig when every single door had a huge yellow triangular sign on it depicting the universal black toilet man walking straight into one.

During this time of domestic unrest, we had a very special visitor on board. It was only a brief visit as he was on his way to Africa via Asia where he would find another rig to rest on. He likes rigs because it's in his nature to claim the highest point on the horizon. And once claimed he will defend it with his life. He is a falcon, a fearsome predator.

In his first week, he killed an owl who dropped in—I presume because it got lost, having been blown offshore in a storm that came through one night—as well as a crow and half a dozen sparrows. The owl was minding its own business on the heli-deck, probably wondering what the big 'H' stands for, when our guest just leaned forward off the railing of the crown block at the top of the derrick and plummeted straight down two hundred feet, whistling past our derrickman's head, wings swept back to reduce drag and increase speed—speed he needed as the owl was much bigger than him. At what seemed like inches from impact into the drill floor, he shot horizontally straight out of our level 'V' door, just a blur, a weightless arrow, down the catwalk and across the heli-deck in seconds. The noise of the rig covered his lightning approach. In the last few feet he threw his legs forward, extended his wings and buried his talons deep into the unsuspecting owl's back. An explosion of feathers erupted as the owl fought back but to no avail, he was already too seriously wounded from the first strike. Our assassin made a meal of the owl and returned to his throne on the crown block. What remained of the owl was given a burial at sea; he never knew what hit him.

At 3 a.m. one morning I was talking to the tool pusher in the 'dog house', the room where the driller stands on the drill floor, when our guest came down from the derrick, flew straight in, and perched himself on a cable in the corner not three feet from my head and went to sleep. Not afraid or even curious, he just got too cold up there, as the wind and rain had been lashing the derrick for several hours now. All week we had been steadily sliding past freezing point, and the temperature would continue to fall past minus fifty as we headed into winter. And after all, it's his rig isn't it? So get the fuck out of the way, I'm coming in.

The tool pusher ran off to the galley to get him some bacon. I ran off to get my camera. I was impressed and named him 'Blitzkrieg'. He was equally impressed with me, and shat on my hard-hat twice that morning.

In the migratory season all kinds of birds come through. When the weather suddenly turned foul a huge swarm of tiny finches, too many to count, diverted to our heli-deck and huddled together against the wind, the horizontal rain buffeting them into one big circle of tiny feathers. Then the sun came out for ten minutes and they started to hop up and down and chirp. But, as if God himself was fucking with them in much the same way we did when trying to run cockroaches to death in the galley at two in the morning by flicking the light switch on and off, it started raining again. The third time the rain and wind disappeared and the sun popped out the finches all went apeshit, hopping about on the heli-deck until one of them lifted off above the rest, his tiny wings flapping like fuck. 'DO WE STAY, DO WE GO . . . OR WHAT?!' he chirped to the others. They launched themselves in complete unison back into the sky and in a few seconds they were just a brown cloud trailing the horizon.

Little sparrows buzzed about down on the main deck, jostling for space around the garbage bins. They regularly got bullied by a crow that arrived from nowhere. His reign over the bins was short-lived, though, as one day he strayed too close to the derrick—that's Blitzkrieg's turf. Once again death from above came hurtling down silent and fast. All that remained were a few black feathers and some blood on the floor by the bins.

Blitzkrieg picked off the odd sparrow, snatching it straight out of the air and devouring it mid-flight. He made endless circles around the derrick, occasionally shouting out a warning to everyone above the blaring rig's white noise. 'Come too close and you're a dead motherfucker,' as the tool pusher translated for me.

I liked Blitzkrieg, he kept it simple. When he's rested up and there's a break in the weather he moves on, making the next leg of his long journey, rig-hopping down the coast past Japan and Korea all the way to Africa. He makes the trip every year, playing 'beat the clock' with the elements, returning to the same rigs again and again. He's warmly received on every drilling derrick from Russia to Sudan. Accepting whatever name they give him, he knows every local custom, speaks a dozen languages. He blends in, disappears into the steel and kills anything that comes too close to his rig. If there was a symbol for our industry, it's him.

IMMBRUIMMBRUIMMBRUIMMBRUIMM

BRUNEI DARUSSALAM

****

ENTRY VISA

Visa no : KB/67 1/99

Reference no : KB/S27/7/96

Category: ~~Single entry~~/multiple entries to Brunei Darussalam not later than 17.5.2000 provided this passport remains valid

For Controller of Immigration Brunei Darussalam

Date: 17 MAY 1999

Fee: $ 30/- Rt. no: 4

VS 02

MALAYSIA IMMIGRATION SG. TUJUH, SARAWAK SOCIAL/BUSINESS VISIT PASS

Reg 11, Imm. Regn. 63

United Kingdom of

Passport

Passeport

Type/Type P

Code of Issuing State/Code de l'Etat émetteur

Surname/Nom (1) CARTER

Given names/Prénoms (2) PA

Nationality/Nationalité (3) BRITISH

Date of birth/Date de naissance (4)

Sex/Sexe (5)

Place of birth/Lieu de naissance (6)

29 MAY 1999

DEPARTED

INTERNATIONAL AIRPORT

IMMIGRATION

BRUNEI DARUSSALAM

2 GET BEHIND ME SATAN

We were more than two months into the job and the well was doing all kinds of shit. We were taking losses. That means all the drilling fluid inside the well was overcoming the formation pressure. With this type of exploration or 'wildcat' drilling, it's always a gamble—over-pressurised formations become really dangerous in these situations.

We kept pumping mud to maintain hydrostatic pressure, but it's sustainable only if crews can keep up the pace of mixing new mud at the same pace that losses occur. We can only produce mud so fast, and 'The Cunt of Monte Christo' could only mix new mud as fast as his spacesuit and bad vision would allow.

The well was taking thirty barrels an hour in losses and it was increasing. If it got above one hundred it was all over.

So we drilled ahead, mixed and pumped mud, keeping a furry eyeball fixed on the digital mud fluid-level gauge like a degenerate gambling junky stares at a roulette wheel in a windowless casino. Just like us he's overtired, jumpy from all the coffee and worried about the loan shark who's going to take his thumbs if he loses.

Our loan shark was the oil company; they had a pretty new logo but would happily drill all the way, indeed into Satan's special 'Beelzebub Reserve', looking for what we call 'shows'—traces of hydrocarbons. The next time we tested the well we were going to knock on Satan's door again; if we got a hit then the dealmakers would keep us in war and V8 supercars for another five years.

The only problem was, we had just hit compressed chert at 2470 metres, one of the hardest rocks to drill through. So the stakes had been raised. If the bit wore out before we were through the chert then we wouldn't have enough chemicals to mix more mud and keep pumping above the losses. And the dealmakers would have to go home and trade in their V8s for public transport.

But after two months of relentless drilling we finally got what we came for. The money men found their hydrocarbons, the chert gave way to soft limestone, we drilled into this formation and started preparing to run casing. After that the well testing would start, and that involved 'flaring' the well.

It's wild when a well flows. A live gas well is a remarkable thing and you're playing a dangerous game with Mother Nature. The gas is very carefully flowed up to the rig, with the aid of enough German über-engineering to relaunch the space programme, and diverted through a long high-pressure armoured hose to a giant arm that hangs over the side of the rig. At the end of the arm lies a directional head with jets jutting out forming a circle around it. The liquid gas flies up the well expanding at an unbelievable rate, the rumble turning into a roar and sending nervous looks in all directions. By the time it has reached the drill floor it's breaking the sound barrier.

In a second it slams into the head, the ports open, the burners ignite, and everyone snatches their whole body back like a collective hand caught over a Bunsen burner as millions of cubic feet of highly volatile liquid gas vaporise and explode, lighting up the night sky in a fireball that sends an invisible shockwave over the rig and makes every living thing in the sea for miles stop and look.

The sound alone is like ten jumbo jets taking off at the same time. The crew run about madly checking and rechecking the heat levels, as a flare boom will peel the paint off the walls and melt your boots to the deck. But all this power flying through the rig is a mere sneeze for Mother Nature—if she wanted to she could spit us into orbit.

'We got a real barn burner here,' said Gerry, the night tool pusher. Gerry knew the rig inside out, back to front and upside down. He's got the power to pull the dragon from the ground, as he liked to put it. He looked down on the rig from the heli-deck, surveying the crew who scurried about trying not to let the rig turn into one giant floating charcoal brick. He smoked his well-chewed cigar through clenched yellow teeth, bending his head down to his hand to do so as forty years of lifting badly has left Gerry with the elbow dexterity of an arthritic ex-tennis pro.

Gerry's old, but he intensely dislikes being told he's an older man. I was in his office one day when the mail bag arrived. He was sitting there thumbing through his correspondence when suddenly he spat his cigar across the desk and started ripping up an envelope. In some insurance form he had been referred to as an 'old age pensioner'. 'I hate that shit, it's like telling you the same Gawd-damn thing three times,' he protested while retrieving his cigar from the small fire it had started in the corner.

'Motherfuckers, I'm still a workin' man,' he mumbled while pouring his coffee over the fire.

The logistics coordinator, Blane, lives in the same state back in the United States as Gerry. I was telling him about Gerry's cigar-spitting tantrum. He laughed and told me about the time he went over to Gerry's cabin in the mountains. Gerry looks like Grizzly Adams would if he'd become really surly and indifferent about his personal hygiene.

It was the middle of winter in Washington State. As Blane walked up to the front door he saw that an entire felled tree was poking through the open doorway and extending some twenty feet into the snow. A tractor was parked with its front end flush up against the end of the tree. Apparently Gerry's chainsaw had broken down so he just pushed the whole fucking tree into the house so the top was jammed into his fireplace, which was directly opposite the front door. As the night wore on Gerry would periodically put down his beer, jump in the tractor and push the tree in another foot as the fire burned down.

It was getting very close to three months since we arrived on the rig. My brain had turned into soup, I was now past it, part of the substructure, the rig had slowly eaten its way into my head like rust on a gangway. I was in the company man's office—he's the one in charge of everything—and he was halfway through the morning meeting. It felt like the millionth morning meeting, and I'd stopped paying attention weeks ago, opting instead to perfect my cow-like ability to sleep while standing up.

All the service company supervisors were packed in, the tool pusher, the petroleum engineer, the mud engineer, the deck pusher, the logistics guy, the directional driller, the sub-sea engineer, the well test supervisor, and the galley boy who had decided to attempt to empty the bin located under the company man's desk was there too—all in a room the size of your average broom cupboard. Everyone else was crammed into the corridor, craning their heads into the office to hear what was going on. Half of the guys looked and smelled like they did most mornings, coming straight to the meeting directly from drool-filled sleep. The rest had coffee and smokes.

Erwin was up on the drill floor running the last well section with the Azerbaijani boys. I knew the end was in sight but after three months I was hopelessly institutionalised; I had to look at the 'ten day operational forecast' printout in my hand just to figure out what day of the week it was.

I wasn't listening; I was having a perverse fantasy involving my girlfriend Clare and a giant beach ball. 'Pauli, how long is it going to take to rig down all your tools, get your manifest sorted, and be ready to go?' asked Colin the company man.

What the fuck? We're still running pipe, I thought.

'Pardon?' I looked back blankly.

'Wake up, mate. All the control lines are installed in the SSSV, tested, the hanger's done and landed, we're going to be laying down your gear soon, so you can hopefully get squared away and be on the chopper at midday. It's the last flight so you either get on it or stay on the rig for the tow down to Korea. So how long to rig down?'

Shit. We had eighteen containers scattered all over the fucking rig, and there were tools, and spare parts, and all kinds of gear from the drill floor to the sack room. And it all had to go back in the right order, in the right container, with the right paperwork. I glanced at my watch. Fuck. It was 7 a.m., and every man and his buddy were going to want to use the crane all day, and there was some very bad weather inbound.

'Three hours,' I said. Fat chance.

I left the meeting, stepped out on deck, pulled up my collar as it was snowing heavily and made for the drill floor. I explained to Erwin that we had to get the square peg in the round hole and do it blindfolded with one hand tied behind our backs. But that didn't matter, I could have said that John Howard was going to be eaten by aliens and Erwin was the only guy who could stop them, and he would have. Because Erwin saw the chopper in his mind, he imagined himself climbing into it, he could see a cooler full of chilled beer being fondled by a big-breasted slightly tacky female co-pilot. It was there within his grasp, the end of the oilfield rainbow, the elusive chopper, the Holy Grail, and the only way to preserve your sanity and get the fuck off the rig.

What happened next is still a mystery to me, but I can say that it was like being part of a massive, synchronised ballet. Every guy could see the end and performed at his best, anticipating his crew member's next move so well it was simply fluid, harmonised, perfect.

Twelve noon rolled around. And we were ready. Somehow everything came together, the oilfield equivalent of a hole-in-one. We even had time to shower and eat something. Had Erwin not been there, though, I'm pretty sure I would have been sitting on that rig all the way down to Korea.

The chopper finally arrived and we all lifted off in rubber survival suits, exhausted and euphoric at the thought of going home. Watching the rig get smaller through the window until it was eventually swallowed by the sea, I felt fantastic. I could have swum back to Australia.

Our chartered fixed-wing flight was on time—another surprise—and by 7 p.m. that night we were all sitting in a bar in Yuzhno-Sakhalinsk. Yuzhno is the biggest town in Sakhalin, an island peninsula running some three hundred kilometres up Russia's north-eastern seaboard, and it's rough, with the highest crime rate in the entire Russian federation, not to mention frequent bear attacks.

Most of the men in the bar sat on stools, nursing

beers and ignoring one another, but my Azerbaijani boys from the rig were already getting out of control. Kamran in civilian clothing looks like a giant silverback gorilla would if someone had snatched it from the zoo, shaved it, taught it basic sign language, dressed it in a bad Hawaiian shirt, stuck a Charlie Chaplin moustache on it and let it loose in a bar full of lumberjacks. Erwin was in the corner watching motorcycle speedway racing with a glass of wine, which tends to put him in a catatonic state. The others were ordering vodka, lots of vodka. Russians are generally traditionalists and with any social interaction old-school rules apply: men pull out chairs for the ladies, hold open doors to let others pass and maintain eye contact when they shake your hand. After the first bottle of vodka is consumed, however, all this degenerates into a kind of giant footy brawl with shooters and lots of incredibly loud, cacophonous singing.

The Russia that ran on fear and secrets ran on vodka too, mind you. Why do you think all the spies in those old 'film noir' movies were always leaning against lampposts in dank Moscow back streets trying to light endless cigarettes with damp book matches? That's right . . . they were hammered on vodka, just like Boris Yeltsin.

Russia is still getting hammered on vodka to the tune of 15 litres a year per person. Except it's a federation now, a federation of quarrelling nationalities forming a big black space in the world map that's entirely full of places ending in 'stan'. In fact, the only consistency left that transcends all former Soviet borders, other than oil, is vodka. Generations of hardened piss-heads survived Stalin, the Nazis, perestroika and, of course, communism on vodka.

The space race ran on vodka. In Star City circa 1965 gallons of the stuff were consumed daily. Launching rockets must be a bit like playing pool: you get better at it after the first drink. The humble potato has been fuelling a powerful toxin since the twelfth century.

From the time we started keeping track of things in Russia, it's been slowly improving. Things are better now than they were only a decade ago. Things are better, actually, than they were at 7 a.m. that morning. As our Western influence—with its drugs, crime, Diet Coke and Levis—creeps from one end of Russia to the next so does the need for the Russian people to see it and live it first-hand. Russia is a place in flux. Go to any of its major cities and you will find all the same distractions you have at home, only they're more expensive, ergo there is a never-ending stream of people waiting to get out. Any random Russian would gladly trade a two-bedroom flat in Moscow for a sleeping-bag in Sydney. And for a great many Russians, having just about anything you ever wanted at your doorstep but knowing you can never afford it is just a bit frustrating. I'm talking about Levis here, not Ferraris. Would the last person to leave please remember to turn off the lights and close the iron curtains?

No matter where you go in Russia you are guaranteed to see three things: the AK-47 assault rifle, too much prefabricated concrete, and a shitload of vodka. Much like the concrete, there is a massive array of different Russian vodkas to try—around sixty-nine brands in total, ranging from the nasty paint-stripper-peel-the-enamel-off-your-teeth vodka to the two-hundred-dollar-a-bottle premium vodka.

According to the Bureau of Alcohol, Tobacco, Firearms and Explosives—which sets the rules for spirits sold in the United States—vodka is defined as a neutral spirit 'without distinctive character, aroma, taste or colour'. Therefore you'd think all vodkas would just taste the same, leaving your 'premium' vodka as a bit of an oxymoron. To me they were all very similar, but hey, I was just happy to be there. You can mix vodka with just about anything or pour it in your lawnmower if you run out of two-stroke. Vodka suits any occasion, goes with any food, and is enjoyed by silverbacks. And is the only alcohol you can store in the freezer because it contains absolutely no water—perfect for rigs in minus-fifty-degree climates and any other frozen place on the planet.

In this particular bar, vodka came in bottles, pots, aluminium canisters—you name it. One was a glass rendition of an AK-47, complete with polished rosewood and red satin-lined presentation box, the muzzle being the pouring end. There were even porcelain nuclear submarines and babushka dolls with disturbing faces (you have to pull their heads off to drink out of them—just what you want to do with a babushka doll). And that night we sampled them all. The best one by far was the black glass missile with a bright red warhead lid appropriately named 'Red Army Vodka'.

On that night, we were drinking vodka from a bottle that after each pour said 'cheers' in Russian by way of a tiny device in the base. As we drank our way down, the electronic voice kept saying cheers in ever-increasing degrees of drunken slur—*Yura, Yura, Yura*—so that by the time we were on the last drop it was just a monosyllabic grunt. This proved to be Kamran's favourite. He danced about to an Elvis song and answered the bottle—all he needed was a banana in his free hand and the picture would have been complete. People didn't know how to react to him; some looked nervously over his huge shoulder as if searching for his handler, others just ran.

Over the years spent on the rigs and in Russian pubs in between I've seen vodka drunk in all manner of interesting ways. There's the 'paper bag full swig from the bottle while urinating on a dumpster' method, a popular one. There's the 'neck a shot immediately followed by a chunk of black bread smeared with caviar' technique, or the 'shot with a whole poached egg'. After a few of those your average hairy Russian man looks like a giant alcoholic hamster who forgot to hibernate. Some vodkas are followed with raw pickled herring on a stick, some are accompanied by chillies or gherkins or both. Some are combinations of all the above . . . and then they set it on fire. That's my favourite. The gentle waft of burned hair mixed with those harsh Russian cigarettes evokes thoughts of the heady days of revolution and cheap rockets.

My crew had just got to the 'setting it on fire and drinking it' stage of the evening. Huge cheers erupted after each shot when the mini inferno was downed by a crew member feeling no pain and the subsequent fire was put out.

'No more setting the drinks on fire,' I eventually protested. It was getting late and at this point we would have been better off just up-ending our shots on our heads and chasing each other about with cigarette lighters. Everyone in the crew was hammered, they could all speak fluent Russian and they were dancing with the locals who, for some reason, were all dressed very similarly; indeed, practically every male was wearing the unofficial uniform of black leather coat, blue jeans and weird pointy black leather 'brothel creeper' shoes. The only colour in the room was worn by the women, who minced about giving everyone their best 'in your dreams' look. Ultra-bright genuine imitation rayon and sequins gave way to turquoise blue combined with scarlet red, the kind of combinations you see when hippy activists try to dress up. And the gear in Russia is badly made, with uneven stitching and heavy coarse materials, and everything bulges in all the wrong places. Think doll's clothes blown up to life-size. Not that this made any difference to the guys after three months offshore.

Erwin appeared through the smoke, talking about motorcycles and drinking on an empty stomach and how he's got me a 'nose bag'. Then he dragged me into a back room, sat me down in front of a wonderful, piping-hot bowl of borsch and disappeared. It's a traditional dish, basically beetroot soup and meatballs sealed with a lid of pastry on top. It's definitely of the poor-man's food variety, the kind found in every Russian household. Winter food, warming, filling and incredibly appropriate, as outside the temperature was sliding past minus thirty-six degrees. And after the crap we'd been getting on the rig, this was manna. I loved it. Slurped and chewed it with all the gusto my inebriated state allowed.

Another member of my Russian crew, Avas, staggered in singing, fell into a chair and slammed a bottle of Absolut onto the table. He ordered a nose bag of borsch from a Russian waitress who looked like a drag queen who had stapled a dead tarantula to each eyelid. The vodka was finished off like an aperitif upon which Avas belched 'AAABSOLUT', banging down the empty bottle and laughing. If only the New York advertising punters could have seen that.

Kamran walloped around the corner, barking something in Russian and pointing a hairy finger at the even hairier waitress. She came over, he sat down and ordered, then looked at me and said 'Ugly girl' loud enough for everyone to hear. I looked around but no-one was listening. Kamran's ability to simply state the obvious was bizarre. He would wander up to me on the rig while I was writing, sit down opposite me and say, 'So you like writing then,' like he had been hypnotised by someone waving a turd to and fro in his face. The waitress was in fact truly horrendous. She looked about as female as Mike Tyson would if he went through his girlfriend's handbag and ate her lipstick.

Avas was trying to negotiate a meatball into his mouth but ended up chasing it across the floor and under a table occupied by two rough, salty-looking Russians. Meanwhile, I was also having some difficulty with a meatball that had landed in my crotch. The two men next to us were not happy with Avas under their table and Russian eyeballs were turning red. Avas banged his head and let fly with a high-speed abusive torrent, and the two Russians stood up, gold teeth gleaming, veins bulging in their leathery necks.

'Oh fuck,' I said and jumped up, sending my meatball flying across the floor. I faked a smile, showing them the palms of my hands. Why didn't I learn all thirty-three letters of the Russian alphabet when I had the chance? One of the boys on the rig had the sort of phrase book you get at school and had tried to teach me some basic sentences. But I never really thought I'd need them so could never be bothered trying.

My brain frantically searched for something and came up with '*Da*'. They glared at me. '*Dobrae utro*,' I added, which means good morning and explains why Boris Yeltsin always went for the hug instead of the talking thing. The two Russians walked over, their gaze fixed and powerful. Then, as if a blockage somewhere deep in my brain burst, I let go with one. 'The dog chased the cat,' I spluttered in Russian.

Kamran defused the fight that was imminent, simply by standing up. Avas emerged from under the table, having retrieved his meatball—and indeed he was eating it—and apologised to the two men, who, having looked long and hard at all three hundred pounds of Kamran, decided that the fight wasn't worth it and left.

Kamran sat down, looking like a disturbed silverback. He wrapped a massive arm around my neck, tapped his finger against his temple, pulled focus on a space three inches above my eyes and told me what the Cyrillic tattoos on his arms meant, then ordered another bottle. This was one of the few times that I felt grateful for his jailhouse tattoos and size—they definitely saved us. I went back to scanning the floor for my meatball, but Avas had already finished it off, greedy bastard.

3-PHILIPPINES 2000.
PHILIPPINES
IMMIGRATION
Date
Status
Stay

折らないで下さい。
カード②は出国時に入国審査官へ
*Please type or print
*Do not fold
*CARD (2) is to be submitted to the
at the time of your departure from

ed Kingdom of Great Britain and
rt Passport

PHILIPPINE IMMIGRATION
Visa Waiver Pursuant to Memorandum
Order No. 04, Permitted stay
up to July 30, 2000
The Commissioner

Type/Type
Surname/Nom (1)
CARTER
Code of Issuing/Code
State
GBR
Given names/Prénoms (2)
Nationality
Date of birth/Date de naissance (4)
Place of birth/Lieu de naissance (7)
Date of issue/Date de délivrance (8)

HIGH COMMISSION FOR BANGLADESH ★ CANBERRA ★

Dep. & Ext. Section

PHILIPPINES IMMIGRATION
ARRIVAL
JUL 2000

3 JUST ADD WATER

My work takes me to some strange places, usually Third World, and often during a coup, jihad, civil war, uprising, or riot of some description. If all that fails to happen then, with my track record, there will be a natural disaster. Only in the oil industry, the messy try-not-to-cut-a-limb-off side of the oil industry, does one realise first-hand that no matter what's going on in the world, the drilling goes on regardless—mind that landmine.

After enduring the sheer madness of Nigeria, getting shot at in the Philippines, being locked up in Vietnam, getting dysentery in Papua New Guinea, suffering the worst toothache of my life in a Russian tundra hundreds of miles from the nearest dentist—oh yes, and there was that whole rig-sinking thing on that last three-month long job—I thought a nice holiday was in order. Europe with its safe civilised streets, what could possibly happen there?

But before my long-awaited holiday could start I had to get some training courses out of the way. I was looking at a very hectic week. Erwin and I arrived back in Singapore looking and feeling like a couple of parolees. After three months on that rig, I realised I had been out there too long; it was definitely fiddling with my sanity. It's the little things that make a difference—after a normal, relatively lucid man has been effectively institutionalised on the rig by the rig system, just walking about in regular clothing feels special and everything your senses experience is welcome. People, traffic, toilet paper that doesn't feel like a lump of coal, toilets that flush instead of trying to suck your guts out of your backside, warm showers, real food, walking more than ten feet in a straight line, lawn—everything.

The following morning was day one of the next job's DWOP—Drill the Well on Paper—meeting. During these meetings everyone involved in the operation, from the brightest minds in the oil world to a third-generation driller with the attention span of a nine-year-old and obvious anger-management problems, sits around in a nice hotel conference room packed with three-dimensional well bore schematics and more laptops than a Tokyo subway and gets blind drunk for three days. If drinking was an Olympic sport these guys would be the best in the world. I'm not quite sure how I survived it, but I did. Just.

Then we headed off for our training courses, one of which required the crew to simulate doing their job on the drill floor while the training staff introduced various problems, up to and including emergency situations, all designed to closely monitor what each individual does under varying degrees of stress. This is done every few years and, since my last visit, the facility had introduced a new safety protocol: heart monitors. This seemed unusual but necessary given that in the previous year some poor sod had too much excitement and dropped dead of a heart attack.

We all lined up while an extremely attractive nurse shaved our chests, taped a small transmitter to the small of our backs and stuck little round suction cups all over us. Two of the other guys had also just come from long jobs offshore. One of them, an American named John, had spent more than two months on a particularly rough rig in Africa and the poor bugger now had to go through all this shit on his own time before he could go home to his wife. I felt sorry for him. He was young and I could see his mind was already home in bed.

The nurse wasn't helping much. John lit up like a Christmas tree when she walked in and started preparing to shave us. 'Gawd-damn,' he said as she bent over to pick up her bag. Her nurse's uniform looked like it had been borrowed from a B-grade porno, and in the right light you could see straight through it. Her serious bedside manner and ample bosom just made it worse. From the look on John's face you'd think she was getting him ready for a lap dance, not an extremely expensive exercise that we all had to pass if we had any chance of working on the rigs again, regardless of how hot the nurse was.

The nurse turned to talk to a doctor who had stuck his head round the corner, allowing all of us to take in her profile. My young friend piped up again, 'Gawd-damn.' I looked at him but he just gave me an ambiguous grin and said, 'She looks like a dead heat in a zeppelin race, man.'

Ten hours later we had finally finished the exercises when a middle-aged man in a white lab coat came tearing up the metal staircase onto the fake drill floor.

'Number five is having a seizure!' he shouted. Somewhere an alarm sounded. 'Where is your number five?!'

Oh shit, who's number five? We all exchanged blank looks. Everyone was on the drill floor. Everyone except John.

The whole crew took off looking for him. I ran into the change room—empty. I looked frantically at the toilet doors and noticed that one of them was closed. I kicked it in and found John with his dick in his hand, no doubt engrossed in some lurid fantasy involving the nurse. 'Nice one, you fuckhead!' I yelled while he tried to shove his boner back in his pants. 'Next time take off the heart monitor first.'

John fumbled to deactivate the black box and promptly dropped it in the toilet.

The next day I was sitting in a departure lounge in Singapore's Changi Airport about to board a flight to London; finally, my happy, quiet, safe holiday could begin. As luck would have it, my arrival in the UK coincided with a wave of terrorist bombings. Only a few hours before we landed, the aircrew had announced that London had succeeded in winning the much-coveted host city campaign for the 2012 Olympics. Now elation had dissolved into horror. The sun was shining as I wandered the streets, but the air was thick with uncertainty and people hurried past me with pained, worried faces. Literally millions were stranded in the city, unable to go home because of the gridlock created by the closure of the underground train system and all the major bus routes.

Within a few hours the streets went from crowded to bizarrely empty. London had been brought to a standstill. I could feel the panic leaching up my spine, and soon I found myself no longer admiring the grand old city buildings but visualising them going from sturdy symbols of culture steeped in rich history to shattered rubble. Britain's backbone could be brought down like New York's by our generation's Achilles heel. Namely some shithead with high explosives strapped to his back. I should have stayed on that crappy rig; I'd be halfway to Korea by now.

I hired a car and waited for the traffic to ever so slowly start moving again. I found the A1 and headed for bonny Scotland; perhaps I would spend the next three weeks in the highlands drinking my favourite single malt. Pitching a tent in the heather and drinking the Macallan all day sounded pretty good . . . Unless someone decided to blow up the entire Spey Valley, I felt confident I would be pretty safe.

Instead I was pulled over for speeding before I'd even reached the city limits. It was nice to see the police officer approaching my car with only a stern expression. Gone are the days when your local 'bobby' carried a truncheon and a whistle in his pocket. Gone forever are the days when a criminal would hear the words 'STOP . . . OR I'LL SAY STOP AGAIN!' as he was pursued down the street by said bobby blowing his whistle while brandishing his truncheon that's about as threatening as your average dildo. Now they carry automatic weapons and only say 'STOP' once. And you'd better stop.

Luckily, in this case, no shots were fired and I ended up having a perfectly excellent conversation with my terribly polite and completely informative constable—yes, strange, even for me. He let me off with a warning, then told me a story about two of his fellow officers that's worth retelling.

One dark and stormy night they were sitting in their police car, close to the Scottish border in Cumbria, patiently waiting for someone like me to drive by a little too fast. It was the dead of night, black as pitch and so overcast there was no moonlight, no ambient light, just the black hills and these two cops sitting in their car with a thermos of hot soup.

Then from the south they heard a screaming high-performance engine. The sergeant got out, grabbed the hand-held speed gun and pointed it into the darkness. The vehicle they both heard shot by them at an unbelievable rate, straight out of the night, doing 190 miles per hour with no lights on at all. Both men stood stumped on what to do next. While they were discussing the matter, the car screamed past them going back the other way at an even faster pace. This went on until a road block was finally set up, to reveal two Tornado pilots in a black Lamborghini with full night-vision helmets on.

I drove on. The A1 had gone from being the biggest carpark in Europe to a fast-flowing motorway, and before long I was in the Cotswolds heading for my sister's place. The last time I dropped in on my sister seven years ago she lived in Dorset, famous for its cider. We spent the day in her local pub, called 'The Headless Woman'. I sat at the bar next to a farmer who looked like he'd just come from Middle Earth and heard all about how, back in 16-something just after the pub opened, the local witch was beheaded on the bar for possessing a cow. He gave me a pint of 'Scrumpy', the local brew, a dark cider that tasted great even though it had toenails floating in it and got me so drunk I passed out tongue-kissing his border collie.

This time we stayed away from the local pub and instead enjoyed a walk in the rolling green hills with my sister's dogs. She has two, both Northern Inuits; basically they're wolves, only they howl more and eat more. At one point I got a stick and instantly became the target. I took off running through a wheat field feeling a bit like Kevin Costner, until they bailed me up and ate my new denim jacket.

In Britain everyone appears to have a dog. The last time I was there almost every street I walked down, from central London to Aberdeen, had a dog turd with my name on it; I spent more time looking at the ground directly in front of me than at the sights. However, this has changed. Britain is poo-free thanks to heavy council fines, and wandering tourists are no longer head-down but are able to zigzag about willy-nilly with a camera permanently pressed to their preferred eye. As a result

I had stupidly developed a false sense of security about all things poo-related.

Consequently, I was a little taken aback a week later while wandering down a crowded Paris street. I was there for only a few days, trying to drum up new business. I left the meeting feeling positive and decided to kill my last few hours watching the fourteenth of July Bastille Day parade.

I stopped, turned to cross the street, and there directly opposite me was a huge Chanel store. Standing in the entrance was an immaculately dressed middle-aged woman holding a delicate silver lead in her gloved hand, attached to which was a spotless white poodle puckering up and attempting to squat, and no doubt eventually shit, right in the middle of the signature black-and-white doormat that probably cost more than my car.

But people wandered past looking relaxed and there was an air of celebration in the city. The French lady politely ignored her poodle, which was punching out the poo of its life. Well-dressed young people stepped over it as they made their way up the expansive marble steps into the Chanel building.

Finally it was over, the little dog bounced up and down with joy next to what looked like its own bodyweight in shit. Then, to my surprise, the lady opened her Louis Vuitton handbag and produced a dainty pink tissue. Oh, I thought, she's actually going to make some sort of effort to get rid of it. I was curious about what technique she would adopt for such a delicate manoeuvre, short of retrieving a shovel from her bag. But, no, she simply bent over and wiped the dog's bum, stuck the tissue on top of the turd and minced off down the street.

I enjoyed the parade. All of France's military might have marched by, gleaming in bright colourful splendour. I left central Paris looking like Ken Done just threw up all over it. Here's a hint: wear your old shoes if you go, and if you visit the Chanel store remember to check the mat before you wipe your feet.

IMMIGRATION SINGAPORE
VISIT PASS
Subject to Reg. 12 (7)
Immigration Regulations

07 JUN 2001

PERMITTED TO ENTER AND
REMAIN IN SINGAPORE
FOR THIRTY DAYS FOR
SOCIAL VISIT ONLY FROM
DATE SHOWN ABOVE.

22 JUN 2001
PERMITTED TO ENTER AND
REMAIN IN SINGAPORE

1 AUG 2001
PERMITTED TO ENTER AND
REMAIN IN SINGAPORE
FOR THIRTY DAYS
SOCIAL VISIT ONLY FROM
DATE SHOWN ABOVE

IMMIGRATION
出国
DEPARTED
入国審査官 日本国
NARITA(1)
26 NOV. 2006
IMMIGRATION

IMMIGRATION AUSTRALIA
2 1 JUL 2001
DEPARTED
AUSTRALIA

DEPARTURE
APR 23 2002

THE UNITED STATES OF AMERICA
VISA
ISSUED AT
LONDON
B-2 4 JUN 1980

4 ENDURING THE RIGGERS

There was a time when I didn't know my father. There was a time when he didn't know me. Now, there's rarely time enough to take a breath between conversations.

He is very happily retired these days, but in his past he was a Royal Air Force squadron leader, and after leaving the service he embarked on an oilfield career that he excelled in, reinventing himself as a directional driller and, by all accounts, a very good one. In his mid-thirties at the time, with my mother and two young children to support, a complete change of career and environment must have been hard to deal with, let alone working on the rigs. I never made the effort to spend any time with him following my parents' divorce when I was nine. And it didn't help when my mother, my sister and I moved from England to Perth when I was fifteen. It is only now, at thirty-six, that I've started to realise what I have missed. He is, after all, my father, and as I discovered on my last visit he has the same interests as I do, indeed he has the same walk when he's pissed, the same laugh and the same ability to fall on his feet no matter how badly he's fucked up. Every now and again I run into an old drilling hand on some rig in the middle of nowhere who knew my father; it's a big industry, global, but within the drilling side it's very small. You can have a bad job one week in the Middle East, and a week later they're discussing it on a rig in Australia.

Dad looked relaxed. A few years had gone by so we had a lot to talk about. I told him about Clare, my girlfriend, and how, despite all the years of listening to horrific divorce stories in locker rooms offshore from here to North Africa, I was ready to ask her to marry me. His response was perfect: 'Marry for love, son, but if she's rich, don't forget your dear old dad,' and with that he burst out laughing. We cracked a bottle of Macallan and talked through the night.

I told him about a motorcycle accident I'd had a few years earlier. The recently restored bike was pristine until I had a classic 'Get Off', sending my bike that had taken two years to complete into a wall, then I went offshore the next day with a cracked rib and large chunks missing from various parts of my body. I nearly lost my job at the time as I had trouble strapping myself into the four-point harness on the chopper in Russia. Dad gave me a hard look, had a sip on his whisky, delivered a brief lecture on late braking and wearing leathers, then launched into a story about the time he decided to ride his Vincent 'Black Shadow' down the hall and through the bar of an Officers' Mess on an air base forty-odd years ago.

He was drunk, but that goes without saying, got as far as the entrance, hammered the throttle, dropped the clutch and just held on, but didn't actually go anywhere. After a couple of seconds he realised that the thirty feet of red hall carpet the bike was sitting on was being hurled out the door and into the carpark by the Vincent's spinning back wheel. Then he ran out of carpet, and the bike shot out from under him and landed in a trophy cabinet halfway down the hall. He was in serious trouble, but landed on his feet.

'Wasn't too long after that when I met your mother in Germany,' he said and smiled, then mysteriously left the room. When he came back he handed me a small velvet box. Inside, twinkling at me, was a beautiful antique engagement ring. 'This is the only engagement ring in the family, son. It's very old, I've been holding onto it for you.'

I told him I was going to Afghanistan to write about the use of private military contractors and oil. He gave me his take on working in that part of the world, as many years ago he had been tasked with finding a flight crew who went down in the desert, and during his time drilling he had worked predominantly in the Middle East. So between his four years running the desert survival school in El Adem for the Air Force and fifteen years on rigs directional drilling in the desert, he had some good advice to give me and a few great stories as well. It wasn't the first time he had suddenly opened up with insights into his past. The last time I was here I had a blast with him and a couple of his mates in London. I was only there for less than a day before the office phoned and told me to go back to the rig, but that short day was one of the best I'd spent with my dad.

Einstein once said: 'Imagination is more important than knowledge. Knowledge is limited. Imagination encircles the world.' My imagination has saved me, and tortured me, but only once did it run away and leave me sitting alone at a table with the only two men who really scared me. It was some ten years ago, and it started on a flight.

'You don't look nervous,' she said with a smile, as we dropped out of the sun and into a typically British winter. I had been calming my nerves by chatting to the woman sitting next to me on the flight. Since we departed Singapore she had regaled me with everything from her messy divorce to her daughter's academic prowess, and even better her ex-husband was paying for her daughter's education. I was starting to appreciate her ex-husband's side of the story after being married to this woman for twelve years. The in-flight movie was *Silence of the Lambs*, and I have to say it had me on edge because there I was trapped in a conversation about how scared she was after watching it. 'It's about time they made a film with a strong female lead who saves the day. I'd like to see my ex-husband in a cell like that one.' The woman was opinionated and annoying in a way that just made you angry enough to fantasise about getting out of your economy-class seat and gaining instant access to first class, pausing on your way through the curtain to blow a raspberry at her.

But she was distracting me from the uneasy nerves that pulled at my gut. Yes, I suppose I didn't look nervous, but nerves turn some people green and others into stand-up comedians. I was doing the latter. She was laughing so much that little bits of spittle would occasionally land on my face, only fuelling my desire to walk off. 'God, that's so funny,' she spluttered, only just managing to stop her false teeth from landing on her tray table.

I gave her a convincing grin and thought about Dad. It was 1997, I was twenty-seven years old, and in a fit of impulse I was about to arrive unannounced in London where I planned to surprise him. We didn't really know each other, but I'd slipped into the past and had forgotten that I was considered a 'grown-up' now. So the nerves that shook me as a boy in the presence of my father seemed to have manifested and turned me into a comedian at the thought of just turning up at his place.

Dad answered the phone in a strong voice, and sounded overjoyed when he heard I would be on the train within the hour. 'I'll be there to pick you up,' he said.

The arrival hall in Heathrow spread out in front of me. All I had was a small grip bag, no check-in luggage, so I was one of the first people to pass through the big automatic doors and get the full onslaught of faces all registering blankly past me. There towards the back was Dad. He had surprised me in return by driving to the airport. He had grown a full beard and turned a little greyer, but otherwise looked happy and relaxed.

The drive to his London flat was filled with long tortured moments of awkward silence. He dropped me off, gave me the once-around his place and was out the door before I could string two words together. I wandered about the flat for a while, a bit baffled, and decided to make a cup of tea. And that's when I saw the half-empty bottle of Macallan on the shelf. I had two big drinks and flopped down on the couch, feeling light-headed. The phone rang. It was Dad. He said he was at his club with some mates and that I should join them. He told me to go into his closet and find a shirt and tie. Seeing nothing for it, I grabbed a cab and was soon standing at the entrance to what looked just like a regular Victorian terrace house. I rang the doorbell and a man in a suit answered, gave me a wormy dyspeptic smile and asked if he could 'help' me. So it would seem that I had just arrived at a gentleman's club in a Billabong T-shirt and jeans, and that's not acceptable attire at a men's club, so he gave me the pleb's one-size-fits-all shirt, clip-on tie and sports jacket combo.

In I went. The building was old and smelled like a church would if the congregation smoked cigars. It was full of middle-aged men sipping brandy who looked over their glasses at me while folding copies of the *Financial Times*. Dad was at the back in the corner with another man. They were just sitting there, looking at a bottle of wine lying over to one side in a silver cradle.

'Nice outfit,' Dad said and shook his head at me. I was introduced to his mate, Mick. He was heavy-set, his nose had been broken a few times, his voice carried a gravelly tone, and he looked me in the eye when I shook his hand. I liked that. He had an Irish accent and could, I was to discover, drink his own bodyweight in alcohol.

Eventually I had to ask about the wine. They had just purchased it at auction. I reached out towards it. 'Please don't do that,' said a sharp pronounced voice from behind me. I can't remember his name, but I nearly jumped when I turned and saw him; he looked just like Hannibal Lecter from the in-flight movie. He gave me a look that ever so discreetly suggested that if I did touch the bottle he would wait until the wine had breathed, then eat my liver. So I just sat there and sipped on my beer.

I had another two beers and, after being offshore on the rig for more than a month prior to this, combined with Dad's whisky, I was suddenly quite pissed. Nevertheless, for all the jokes and stories I could feel something else going on, like I wasn't supposed to be there. I'd been around some heavy guys on the rigs by that time, older men who included me in the conversation in the bar after the job but not yet to the point of telling me who they were plotting against. I could smell the same guarded undertone here; there was a slightly sinister edge to the table, and I felt like I'd just interrupted their plot to do a bank job or something. We continued with polite conversation that passed the wait, the wait for the 'Corker'.

'He's a specialist, and besides I want to see his technique.' Dad was making no sense to me as he chatted with the others. What the fuck is a 'Corker'? I was thinking.

Dr Lecter picked up on the giant question mark above my head as he puffed occasionally on the end of his cigar. He leaned in towards my right ear and said, 'The Corker will be here soon. He will open the bottle using his own method ... that will be as entertaining as it is rewarding. Clarice, would you like to try the brandy?'

Fuck, he sounds just like him too. I was having déjà vu. And did the motherfucker just call me Clarice? I nodded at him.

'This really is a special day, young Paul.' The Doctor had a thin smile and a bright gold pin buried in the middle of a dark red neck tie. I felt like the prey before the giant angler fish, caught in the twinkle of bio-luminescence before death. 'Do you have your father's passion for single malts?' He poured me a glass of brandy and pushed it across the table.

'Thank you, yes, I love it. I always pick up a bottle duty-free when I crew-change back home,' I said. The brandy tasted like money. I don't belong in here, I thought.

'I've known your father for many years. You're a lot like he was at your age. I suspect working on the rigs agrees with you. He was also an adventurous soul in his past, although now, I dare say, he's slowed down a bit.'

'I'm not running the London marathon, but I'll kick your arse any time,' Dad said and grinned over the table at Dr Lecter, who smiled and shucked the end off a thin cigar. He replaced the silver cutter back in his black waistcoat pocket and struck a match.

'He still figures largely in your value system, even though you have not spent much quality time together.' The cigar spat flames from its end as the Doctor puffed and rolled it around between pursed lips. I was mesmerised.

'What line of work are you in?' I changed the subject and finished another brandy, banging the glass down on the table by accident.

'I was in the service with your father, and now I practise medicine.'

'Oh really, what kind?' I tried to sound sober.

'Psychiatry,' he said.

Oh Christ. Do you eat people? I wanted to say. And why aren't you locked up in a perspex-walled dungeon? This was entirely too weird.

'This is a celebratory drink, a one of a kind, for a one-of-a-kind criminal. It's good you arrived like this. Why don't you tell him now, Allan?' he eyeballed Dad.

Dad stopped talking and suddenly became serious. He looked across the room. 'The Corker's here,' he said.

My jaw slightly agape, I swivelled my head in the direction of the door. There stood a middle-aged short, balding man in a blue suit. He saw us and smartly walked over. In his right hand he held an old-fashioned black leather doctor's bag.

'Good afternoon, gentlemen,' he quipped as the bag's catch sprang open. His hands, manicured and soft, laid out a series of objects in a well-rehearsed method.

'We're so glad you could come. Can we offer you a drink?' asked Dr Lecter.

'Thank you, no,' replied the Corker.

'This is something you won't see very often, Paul.' Dad leaned back in his tub chair as if he was about to get a lap dance.

The table was cleared of empty glasses, and on it sat a Bunsen burner connected to a small silver gas canister, a French garrotte of platinum wire, and a high ball of ice water, into which the Corker coiled up a pheasant feather.

His tools ready, the Corker carefully slid the bottle in its cradle so it sat directly in front of him. The wine was French, if memory serves, a 1945 Château Pétrus—not that it meant anything to me at the time. I just wanted to see how this little fat man was going to open the bottle with the assorted kit on the table in front of him. Especially the feather, couldn't wait to see what he did with that feather.

What did Dr Lecter mean by criminal? Who's the criminal? I didn't know it, but I was about to have the best time I'd had in years, with these characters. I later learned that the celebration was due to the three of them successfully tracking down a particularly nasty con artist who had taken an elderly friend of theirs, Bill, to the cleaners. Once a mountain of a man, Bill had become frail and his wife had passed away. Susceptible and in bad health, he had been duped in the worst possible way. The poor old boy had bought into the con, and as a result he had lost his life savings, his home, even the car. The con was clever, but this time it was played out on the wrong man. Dad, Mick and Dr Lecter, all ex-military, financially independent and bored silly, decided to go after the bastard. They had a real soft spot for Bill, himself a decorated veteran of the worst parts of World War II. The con man was systematically tracked from Dorset in England's south all the way to the north of Scotland, where they eventually caught up with him, in disguise, his features changed and posing as a priest in a small town. They recouped Bill's savings, his house was saved, even the car was returned. The con man had an epiphany, no doubt at the thought of Dr Lecter making soup out of his brain, and turned himself in, God bless him, and as I understand it he's still languishing in prison. Bill has since departed our world, but I know he went with his affairs in good stead and a smile on his face.

The cigar Dr Lecter gave me was making my head feel five pounds lighter, and I forgot the whole 'don't inhale' thing. Nimble fat little fingers adjusted the flame jetting from the tip of the Bunsen burner, heat sending invisible waves into the air that distorted Dad's face across the table. I laughed, but it turned into a cough. 'He's turning green,' Mick said and looked at the Doctor, but he was fixed on the Corker's hands slowly winding his fingers around the polished wooden ends of his wire garrotte. He pulled the wire taut with a 'twang', looked at me briefly and started to heat the wire in the flame until it glowed white hot.

'How's that cigar, Paul?' I heard the Doctor ask me through the brown cloud around my head.

'It's great,' I replied, my head swimming in cotton wool. 'Cheers.' My glass bounced off his with an unmistakable crystal 'ping'. The brandy was like slipping into a warm bath.

'Was it rolled on the thigh of a pretty girl?' I asked. I'm used to Marlboros and Mekong whisky in the back room of some oilfield bar while semi-naked dancing girls gyrate up and down on a pole. Instead, I was sitting there in London in the middle of the old-boy network, drinking vintage brandy and puffing on Cuban cigars while a little bald man opened a bottle of wine with a feather . . . oh yes, the feather.

Once the platinum wire was ready, the Corker wrapped it once around the glass neck, pulling it taut, then in one fluid move he dropped the garrotte and pulled the feather from the glass. It sprang into a metre-long rainbow of wet icy colour that he gently stroked across the hot neck of the bottle. It literally jumped apart, the little man catching the severed top in his free hand. I picked up the top of the bottle; the glass was perfectly cut. The top had been dipped in wax, but I could see the cork inside and it looked intact. The Corker packed up his tools, bid us good day, turned on his heel and was gone. His job was, evidently, done.

I was on a rig a week later telling the story to some mates, who grabbed a blow torch and some baling wire and set off to try it out. It didn't work.

The wine was savoured and sniffed, held up to the light and rolled about on tongues. I stuck to the brandy, the wine would have been wasted on me anyway.

Dad was enjoying himself. He came back from the bar with a bottle of Macallan and before long I was hearing stories.

There were three that I have never forgotten.

15 FEB 2006
PERMITTED TO ENTER AND REMAIN IN SINGAPORE FOR THIRTY DAYS FOR SOCIAL VISIT ONLY FROM DATE SHOWN ABOVE.
Type/Type
Code of Issuing State/Code de l'Etat émetteur
Surname/Nom (1)
CARTER
Given names/Prénoms (2)
Nationality/Nationalité (3)
Date of birth/Date de naissance (4)
Sex/Sexe (5)
Place of birth/Lieu de naissance (6)
Date of issue/Date de délivrance (7)
Date of expiry/Date d'expiration (9)
IMMIGRATION AUSTRALIA
19 AUG 2005
DEPARTED
SYDNEY AIRPORT 3480
UNITED KINGDOM
Name of bearer
Nom du titulaire
Accompanied by spouse
Accompagné de son épouse
and by
et de
National status
Nationalité
BRITISH CITIZEN
No. of passport
No. du passeport
Attention is drawn to the notes
Authority/Autorité
AUS
Holder's signature/Signature
QUESTURA DI ROMA
Visto
valido per mesi
Autorizzazione
Roma
CARTER<<PAUL<
IMMIGRATION
21 AUG 2005
SINGAPORE
Subject to Security
19 AUG 2005
QUESTORE
PERMITTED TO ENTER AND REMAIN IN SINGAPORE FOR THIRTY DAYS FOR SOCIAL VISIT ONLY FROM DATE SHOWN ABOVE.

5 THE OLD MAN

It was 1960, my father was a navigator in the RAF, flying on B Flight of 3 Squadron based at RAF Gelsenkirchen in West Germany. It was there that he met my mother, but that's another story. At the time, he was flying the Javelin Mk 5 all-weather night fighter, a delta wing two-seat interceptor which flew in the 1950s and 1960s. It was B Flight's turn for night flying, and Dad and his pilot, Lieutenant Bill Swettenham, flew a routine sortie of practice interceptions through the early evening of a cool clear April dusk. Later in the night they were briefed for a second mission, where they would go up with another Javelin and practise interceptions, taking turns at being the target. The flight commander, Squadron Leader Peter Stark, was the leader in the other Javelin, with Flight Lieutenant John Lomas in the back cockpit.

Dad was young and full of beans, this was his first operational flying tour, he loved his job and really enjoyed the challenge of chasing unseen targets on airborne interception radar. His face lit up with recall as the ashtray became Stark's Javelin in his right hand with Dr Lecter's silver Dunhill lighter in pursuit between his thumb and index finger. This night was good, Dad said, the weather was excellent, visibility eight miles with minimal cloud cover, and the two jets played cat and mouse for almost an hour. It was during their return or 'recovery' to base that problems for the leader began to show. Interceptions were completed at height in those days, as the potential threat came from high-level Russian bombers. The procedure for recovery was to return overhead to base at height, in this case about forty thousand feet, go into a dive circle, then the first aircraft would dive more steeply in the direction opposite the active runway to about ten thousand feet while the second aircraft would complete one orbit in the dive circle and follow the leader down two minutes later. This separation was made so that the aircraft would land separately two minutes apart, giving the controllers maximum practice.

Dad and Bill were halfway down the dive descent behind the leader when he transmitted a short, garbled radio call to the tower saying that he had serious hydraulic problems and that two of his three hydraulic pumps had failed.

'Pumps one and three,' said Mick and winked at Dad.

'That's right.' Dad looked back at me. I was keeping up with the story so far but it had suddenly got a bit technical, as these stories sometimes do.

Dr Lecter's gold pin drew closer. 'If Squadron Leader Stark had lost his number two and three pumps, then he would have lost all his flying controls and immediately ejected.'

'Right again.' Dad was back on the ashtray with the Dunhill closing fast. So John and Peter were now hurtling towards Earth with only half their flying control, making the aircraft soft to handle and very slow to react. Peter no longer had airbrakes, flaps, undercarriage lowering or wheel brakes for landing.

Peter Stark was a big man. South African by birth, he had joined the SAAF in World War II and had extensive flying experience. 'He was imperturbable and only spoke when he had something to say,' the Doctor said as he put his feet up, leaned back in his chair and disappeared into a cloud of cigar smoke.

'Indeed,' Dad agreed, 'and right now he was busy. We used our airbrakes to control speed on the descent, but Peter was going in hot. Although he got a good radar pick-up and clear directions to the airfield, he had no flaps to limit his approach speed.

'Without hydraulics to lower his undercarriage, he had used the emergency air bottle provided for this eventuality to get his wheels down, but once they are down the wheels cannot be raised again, even on the ground.'

The lead Javelin's radio contacts were infrequent and broken, but Peter managed to touch down just after midnight on runway 27 heading west. 'Just how fast Peter was going must be left to conjecture but he landed bloody fast,' Dad said. 'Our normal touchdown would be around 145 knots. I reckon he was at more than twice that speed. He literally had no means of slowing down and must have been worried that pump two might also fail at any time. If that happened he would have been too low to eject. The relief must have been massive when he knew he was on the ground.'

'At least he was on the deck, but how do you stop a seventeen-ton fully armed jet that's running out of runway?' asked Mick.

'You don't,' said the Doctor. 'You get out of the fucking way.' He was laughing.

'There's an emergency braking lever back on the left side of the cockpit,' said Mick.

Dad nodded sagely and said, 'Yeah, Bill and I were flying alongside Peter at two hundred feet, we were right next to him as he touched down and hurtled down Gelsenkirchen's main runway in the dark, heading for Holland. Bill and I knew Peter would be reaching back frantically pulling on the emergency brake lever. In the event, when he pulled the lever the remaining pressure just bled through the leak that happened during the flight when a union failed. So there were Peter and John, they hadn't slowed down at all, completely out of control doing three hundred knots down the runway with no way of stopping and literally going west.

'We watched him shoot off the end of the runway at flying speed. Bill said, "I guess the emergency brake didn't work." Then Bill broke off and banked hard, executing a remarkable landing on a parallel peri-track.'

Dad and Bill landed without incident, climbed out of their aircraft and ran over to the squadron hanger, only to discover that nobody had realised Peter and John had just started an off-road trip through the German countryside. They had made no further radio calls and the tower personnel didn't notice that they never taxied past.

'I called the ops desk to alert fire and ambulance crews and the CO,' Dad went on. 'Then Bill and I grabbed a Land Rover and took off after the boys. We soon found a bloody huge hole in the boundary fence, and all the approach lights for runway 9 were smashed to bits.

'Peter and John would have just sat there in the cockpit as one of Her Majesty's very expensive brand new aircrafts ran on and on through the German countryside. Peter could not raise the undercarriage as the emergency air system he used to blow down the wheels prevented this, so they went on like that for more than two kilometres.'

Following the Javelin's path, Dad and Bill drove on in the dark, through several large fields, finding large stone walls demolished and the occasional, surprised, slightly scorched sheep, through an orchard, through someone's garden. Peter and John had passed through the greenhouse, through the garage, collected the washing and the washing line, then through another wall into the carpark at the rear of a pub. By chance the port wingtip had taken a few bricks out of the corner of the pub, sending the jet into two parked cars and turning it around towards the building across the street where it lurched over a ditch, losing its wheels, and finally came to rest in a wood directly opposite the pub.

Miraculously, no-one was hurt.

I fell back laughing. 'Go on, then what happened?' I leaned in.

'Peter and John didn't realise it but they were now in Holland,' Dad continued. 'Peter, disoriented after his cross-country rampage, jumped out leaving John to stay with the jet, then he took off heading east to get help.

'All the locals came staggering out of the pub—they had been in there all night drinking and had just heard seventeen tons of aircraft thunder pass, still at some speed. One of them pointed out that his car was missing, then noticed the missing bricks. Of course, they all assumed that John, who was sitting on the ground near the road, was the pilot and had shown great skill in avoiding the pub in the dark. They ran over and the publican gave John a bottle of Dutch gin to steady him and to thank him for his heroism. John knocks off the whole bottle—he doesn't speak a word of Dutch, he's just happy to be alive—and lets them pick him up on their shoulders and dance about on the road.'

That's when Dad and Bill reached the back of the pub, nearly knocking over Peter who was running back down his trail of destruction. Peter got in the car, and when they drove round the corner they saw John enjoying an impromptu street party.

The fire engines, ambulances, and everyone else including the station commander—in full dress uniform—arrived shortly afterwards. 'The station commander at that time was Group Captain Desmond Hughes DSO DFC AFC,' Dad explained, 'a most impressive officer who was generally admired by all under his command. He had been a pilot in the Battle of Britain, his wartime record was superb and he went on to command RAF College at Cranwell.

'A huge crowd had gathered around John and us. The commander stepped forward. He had seen the downed aircraft in the wood on its belly, obviously a write-off. Even then the loss of our latest warplane would have been considerable to the RAF and the United Kingdom at large.

'In his deep, powerful voice, the commander asked John, "My boy, what have you done?"

'Standing there in his flying suit, helmet in one hand, empty bottle of gin in the other, John saluted and said, "I'm sorry, sir, but I've drunk the whole bottle."'

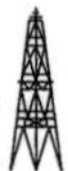

With half the bottle of Macallan gone, we were all laughing loudly, and some of the other men in the club had joined us to listen to Dad's stories.

The next yarn followed soon after. It was less than a year after Peter Stark's crash, and all the same guys were still flying at RAF Gelsenkirchen in the same Javelins. There were two marks of aircraft, the Mk 4 and Mk 5, but the main difference was the size of the fuel tanks and therefore the range. As they routinely flew in pairs, the ops desk tried to give each pair the same mark so they flew together for the whole mission, and on those occasions when different marks came up at the same time, the longer range Javelin 5 would go up first, followed ten minutes later by the Javelin 4, which would join up for the main sortie.

One Monday morning in May, Dad and his pilot were briefed to fly with Brian Mason and Bish Siviter. Brian and Bish were among the squadron's most experienced crews, and they had already completed four night-fighter tours when they joined 11 Squadron. And they were brothers-in-law. Ten years earlier Bish had married Brian's sister, and they had been flying together ever since. Brian was allocated a Mk 5 Javelin and Dad had the Mk 4. The plan was for Brian to take off first, then Dad would follow and join up ten minutes later. So Dad and his pilot were in the hanger checking the aircraft paperwork with two ground staff when Brian started up his port engine.

Cartridges were used to fire up the engines; a slow burning cordite charge would take about eight seconds to spin a small six-foot turbine up to fifty-five thousand rpm. This was geared down to the main engine rotor, and when that was running at two thousand rpm the fuel injectors would squirt fuel into burn chambers, and electronic igniters would fire the fuel and start the engine.

It had rained over the weekend and everything was really sodden. They heard Brian start his ignition sequence in the background as they poured over their paperwork in a small hut at one end of the hanger, then suddenly a massive bang.

'The first thing I remember was the sound of really fast-moving metal fragments ricocheting off the ground,' Dad said, 'and a moment later that horrible "Woooof" of a fuel fire.'

Trained to react in an emergency, all four men yelled 'Don't panic' and ran into each other. Then they all peered round the open door of the hut, and what they saw was frightening.

The starter turbine had disintegrated at maximum rpm, and the tiny blades had torn the collector fuel tank in half and set it ablaze, dumping burning jet fuel under the aircraft and starting a serious fire in the middle of a row of shiny, new, multimillion-dollar jets. The warrant officer grabbed the phone to call the fire section under the tower a few hundred yards away. The sergeant took a small trolley fire extinguisher and charged across the tarmac to help the ground crew. With great presence of mind Dad's pilot sprang into the aircraft next to the one on fire, quickly started it and moved it forward to safety, at the same time making room for the fire engines.

Meanwhile, the Javelin Mk 5 was completely covered in flames, and it was fully armed and very dangerous. Apart from the seven tons of fuel it carried, there were eight hundred rounds of 30-mm cannon shells and four live air-to-air missiles.

Dad ran to the edge of the fire. He could see Brian and Bish inside the cockpit, frantically trying to get out before they either burned alive or just went bang. Ejector seats weren't an option; they would just send them into the hanger roof at a rate that would have the ground crew hosing them into the nearest drain.

Normally in these situations the navigator would just jump off the back of the aircraft, leaving the pilot sole use of the ladder. But the flames, burning over the wings and all around the back of the jet, made this impossible. The only remaining escape route was forward. Suddenly, Bish the navigator was free of the perspex canopy covering the back cockpit, he shot a glance over his shoulder and saw only flames, so he clambered forward and dove off the nose of the jet. His old pal and brother-in-law Brian had shut down the engine, closed the fuel cocks and switched off the electrics. As the fire engines arrived he was sliding down the ladder to escape the flames.

'The next thing I remember was the post-mortem in the aircrew room in the hanger,' Dad said, finishing his whisky. 'Everybody who was anybody was gathered around the table, the room was packed. The fire had been put out by four fire tenders covering the aircraft in foam. A doctor was bandaging Bish's ankle, as he had sprained it leaping from the nose of the jet ten feet up.

'There was Group Captain Hughes again, asking questions. "What did you do after you climbed out of the rear cockpit?" he asked Bish.

'"Sir," replied Bish, "I climbed into the fixed combing between the two cockpits and helped my pilot out of his cockpit, then I jumped from the front of the aircraft, Sir."

'After a short silence, Brian turned to his navigator and asked, "What was it you did after climbing onto the fixed combing?"

'Bish looked his pilot and brother-in-law in the eye and said, "I helped you out of your cockpit."

'There was another short silence, then Brian lent down to reach under the table to pick up his flying helmet. He placed it in the middle of the table so that everyone in the room could see it. There was a size ten, half-melted rubber boot print right across the top of it.'

Dad was on a roll. I was captivated and happy that I was there to see all the boozing and storytelling, the benefits of a classical education displayed with real panache after drinking so much. It made me wish that I had gone to university, back when it was free. Now I suppose if you wanted to eat two-minute noodles and spend the rest of your life in debt, university could be a good idea. But while some of my friends were at uni, I was happy to work offshore. I was still interested in the life the rigs held up, the random adventure was fine with me.

'Let's eat,' said Mick as he stood up. 'What do you feel like?'

We all looked at the Doctor as if he would suggest the best place in London to enjoy a sautéed human hand.

We went through the city in a black cab; it was getting dark and people were starting the journey home. The taxi pulled up outside a French restaurant with long wooden tables outside and starched white tablecloths that clipped against the breeze. It was just opening.

'I love this place. Have the rabbit, it's the chef's speciality.' Dr Lecter looked excited and waited for us to enter through the old wooden doors.

After a while I got my second wind, like drinking yourself sober. 'What happened after Germany?' I asked my father.

'I was posted to Singapore, still on Javelins,' Dad replied.

Then over dinner I heard all about Gus, a young pilot who had befriended my father years earlier after Dad crashed in a paddock in the Welsh mountains—a paddock that belonged to Gus's father. Apparently on seeing a jet crash into his field, he went running up and pointed a shotgun at my father in case he was a German; though the war had ended some years prior to this, life in the Welsh mountains moved at a slower pace in the 1950s. Gus was amazed when he saw the downed jet. My father asked to use the phone to call for help, but it was going to take some time, so he sat down in the farmhouse and got talking to Gus and his dad. They stayed good friends from then on. Gus later went off to join the RAF and did very well, becoming a pilot and eventually flying Javelins in the same squadron as Dad.

Tragically, while they were based in Singapore, Gus was killed after ejecting from his aircraft at low level. As the squadron leader, Dad was tasked to fly Gus's remains back home to the Welsh mountains. Dad was driving down Bukit Timah Road in a Leyland Mini staff car—Gus had been cremated and was in an urn sitting on the back seat—when he hit a wooden cart being pulled by an ox. Dad broke his nose on the steering wheel and the urn slammed into the dashboard, knocking its lid off and turning Gus into one giant grey cloud that filled the Mini and sent my father coughing into the street. Blood pouring from a smashed nose, Dad did his best to scoop his old friend back into the urn, but after the wind had gone through the little car there wasn't much more than a finger or two left in the urn.

Dad made it to the airport, boarded the flight and chain-smoked a carton of Rothmans, ashing into the urn all the way to London. What ended up sitting on the family's mantle for years was mainly cigarette ash; most of Gus went down the road. It took Dad years to tell Gus's father what had happened, and the real reason why he arrived at the remote farmhouse in the middle of the night with blood all over his uniform.

We had dessert, the waiter taking good care of us, and one after another the stories came out.

'I was flying with your dad in the back seat once,' the Doctor said. He loosened his red tie and let a smile spread over his face. 'He had constructed this extendable arm from meccano, and on the end was the hand from a first-aid dummy with a flying glove on it. As a pilot, you'd be bombing along when your dad would stretch this thing out and say, "Excuse me," and tap you on the shoulder with this thing. It's impossible to reach that far forward in the cockpit, so when this hand reaches over and taps you on the shoulder mid-flight you fairly shit yourself.'

Meeting Mick and the good Doctor was superb fun. Seeing them bounce off my dad and being there for the resulting hilarity opened up my feelings towards my father and gave me a better idea of the kind of man he is. And after hearing him talk about his father and the way things were at that time in Britain, I had a new understanding. From that moment on I have had regular contact with Dad, even though it is usually just a phone call. That was enough for us to start again at being a son, and a father.

BRUNEI DARUSSALAM

ENTRY VISA

Visa no : KB/67/99

Reference no : KB/52717

Category: Single entry/multiple entries

to Brunei Darussalam not later than 17.5.2000 provided this passport remains valid

For Controller of Immigration Brunei Darussalam

Date 17 MAY 1999

Fee: $30/- Rt. no: 4

VS 02

MALAYSIA IMMIGRATION
SG. TUJUH, SARAWAK
SOCIAL/BUSINESS VISIT PASS

Passport

Passport

BRUNEI DARUSSALAM

Type/Type

Code of Issuing State/Code de l'Etat emetteur

Surname/Nom (1)

Given names/Prénoms (2)

Nationality/Nationalité (3)

BRITISH

Date of birth/Date de naissance (4)

Place of birth/Lieu de naissance

Sex/Sexe

INTERNATIONAL AIRPORT

6 THE TENDER TRAP

Shortly after I returned from London, I was in Perth for a month, working in an oilfield workshop. Tasman Oil Tools had the contract to service a new Top Drive running tool that I was very interested in, partly because it's a new design that actually works and partly because, if it keeps working, it's going to replace me one day. So I wanted to 'know thine enemy', and after a phone call to Ross, the director, I found myself eye to eye with the thing. It was painfully simple, easy to rig up and I even liked the colour. Bad news.

'Not much to it really,' said Ross. He had done me a favour by putting me on his workshop crew as I was in need of a pay cheque, and he was happy to have someone on hand who knew their way around drilling tools. Ross is a great guy; he has that rare ability to work alongside his employees. He would pass the workshop, see something that didn't look right, and before you could say 'Ross I can't get this fucking thing back together', he would have his shirt sleeves rolled up and be scanning the bench for the right tools.

I enjoyed working there—the crew were great and they got along well with each other. The Russian rig aside, I'm more used to working for your classic, large, eco-friendly oil consortium. The ones who plant a tree for every well they drill and put an overpriced supermarket into every one of their petrol stations. They, along with car manufacturers, dump hundreds of millions of dollars into research towards new energy—hydrogen, nuclear, or mining Australia's vast uranium reserves—without making too much noise. But underneath all the environmentally friendly wallpaper and glossy corporate brochures, they're usually just another conglomeration of ruthless and aggressive bullies, located in a tall, imposing building down town. While I was at Tasman enjoying the workshop life, just such a giant oil consortium phoned, and predictably I said, 'Sure, I'd love the job,' and within twenty-four hours I was on hypocrite airlines bound for Japan.

The rig was just outside Iwamizawa, a small town one hour by train from Sapporo on Japan's northernmost island of Hokkaido. I love working in Japan, it's so clean and polite. When I arrived, it was the middle of winter. Coming from a Western Australian summer it was cold, really cold, the kind of cold that freezes your snot and makes your balls shrivel up and disappear in desperate search of some warmth. So I spent the first few days wrapped in layer upon layer of clothing, looking a bit like the Michelin man, until I slowly got used to the temperature.

The job started well. We had a new computer system on the drill floor that looked impressive, with just the right amount of lights, bells and whistles to attract every Japanese guy on location with even the slightest interest in computers to the drill floor like sociopaths to the 'Big Brother' house. But you can't trust computers. As if on cue, just as I had an assorted plethora of excited high-level Japanese oil company men in hard-hats and matching thermals crowded around our new computer, chatting, pointing and asking an unbelievable amount of questions, it turned itself off.

Fuck, aw fuck, I was shouting in my head, all the while smiling the idiotic way you do when something stops working at a critical moment and you have no idea how to fix it.

The Japanese consortium said 'Ohhhh' in unison and nodded.

Jake, my derrickman, walked over and pulled off his hard-hat and balaclava. 'What the fuck's wrong with it?' He knew as well as I did that after fifteen minutes we had to pay for the rig's time; if you can't fix the problem in that time and you don't have a spare unit then you get the bill for the down time. Time is money in drilling. If the rig stops, someone has to pay.

'I've no idea, it's the new system,' I hissed through my teeth. Through the freezing wind and snow I felt my cheeks burning and could see lots of Japanese eyes checking watches. Your time starts now.

'So can you fix it?' asked Jake.

'I know how to run the damn thing, but not how to troubleshoot it. Send two guys down, unpack the backup, you rig this one down, I'll get on the phone.' I could feel the panic rising in my throat like hot lava, but I knew that I had to keep on smiling and pretend like hell that I knew exactly how to get this thing going again.

Jake turned on his heel and waded through the crowd of snap-happy Japanese guys. The crane was already booming over our spares container. I checked my watch; I had ten minutes to fix this computer.

A big white phone sat in the middle of the tool pusher's desk. I pulled off my hard-hat, balaclava, gloves, goggles and unzipped the front of my jacket, then sat down, thumbed through my tally book, found the 'don't panic' number and dialled. Instantly someone answered. I had no idea what time it was in Houston, but it was like calling the White House situation room. I was asked my name and where I was calling from, what job I was on, what the problem was, and bang, I was transferred to some guy in R&D—reserve and development—in Louisiana.

With the manual in one hand and the phone in the other, I tried to stay calm as the R&D guy who invented the new computer suggested more and more unconventional solutions.

'We've never tried this before, okay, but just take the cover off the back, strip out the main power supply wires and plug it straight into the rig's power supply. Phone me back, let me know what happens, oh, and make sure you earth everything. Bye.' Click.

I looked up to a room full of curious Japanese men with cameras. It didn't take long but after a few minutes the computer was no longer an innovative, shiny thing symbolising all that is new in drill floor electronics. Instead, with all the cables and wires spilling out in every direction, it looked more like a scale model of the human intestinal tract.

I threw the switch and thank fuck it worked.

The Japanese consortium said 'Ahhhh' in unison, then it turned itself off again. 'Ohhhh,' they said.

I rigged up the backup unit, but it failed to start.

'Time,' said Jake as he followed me into the tool pusher's office, kicking the snow off his boots. 'You're supposed to be able to fix all our tools,' he added helpfully, lighting a cigarette.

'Well, I can't fix it this time,' I said, then picked up the phone and started dialling.

'Now we just look fucking stupid.' He glared at me across the small portacabin and sucked on his smoke.

'I'm going to sort this computer bullshit out,' I said firmly. I even convinced myself.

'So it didn't work Mr Carter?' the R&D guy asked, sounding as if he already knew it wouldn't and was waiting for my call.

'Oh hi, no it didn't work.' There was a pause, then he told me his last-ditch idea and said he hoped I would have 'a nice day'.

I slammed the phone down and walked back outside. When I got to the drill floor the boys were standing with the Japanese guys, all taking photos of each other. I did what the R&D guy suggested, and thank whoever it was that decided to give me a break, it worked.

'Ahhhh.'

I love working in Japan. Our clients didn't charge us for the down time, they helped us rig down after the job and offered us *sake* while we waited for the car. They organised all seven of our heavy containers to be returned to Singapore. They were polite, organised, and not one person said fuck, not even in Japanese.

The day after the computer incident, I left the 'bullet train' and the crew in Tokyo, and passed the wait for my flight to Australia via Singapore alone. I wanted to take time out to see a bit of Tokyo. I really love it. Love the graciousness of the old folk, the well-mannered way they welcome you and make you feel like you're all-important, and the complete wildness of the young kids with their crazy Americanese fads and fetishes. I went for a walk in the city's largest park, Mizumoto. It's huge, with long sprawling vistas making seamless transitions into boardwalks that hover over mirrored water from the Edo River. It was weirdly empty and completely peaceful. I spent the day covering as much of Tokyo as I could, unable to resist visiting my favourite places.

Since I was a kid I've collected knives. My dad gave me a pocket knife when I was about eight, and the first thing I did was cut myself, then I whittled down the leg of our coffee table. Some people accumulate stamps, coins or porcelain figurines. I'm into bikes and knives—go figure. Anyway Japan is the home of some of the most remarkable edged weapons. The deputy head of 'All Japan Swordsmiths Association', Shoji Yoshihara, makes possibly the finest blades in the world. He has been designated an important living cultural property of the Katsushika ward, which is the suburb of Tokyo where he lives. He made his first Katana sword at age twelve, studying the art at his grandfather's side. Making a sword the old-fashioned way, by hand, from scratch, from raw materials, takes time and supreme skill. Generations of craftsmen pass on their knowledge to the next generation, their entire lives devoted to the process. I find it fascinating. Yoshihara's blades bear his family's maker mark, 'Kuniie III'. Slipping one out of its *nebukuro* (sleeping-bag) reveals six months of solid work. Its graceful lines suggest only art; however, in the hands of a trained man this blade could easily pass through a human body. This is no letter opener, and at forty thousand dollars I handle it with extreme care.

Bikes and knives provide me with distraction. When I'm at home I'll spend hours tinkering on my bikes. It helps me think. And I've had a lot to think about. Putting the sword down I found myself retrieving the ring Dad gave me; I had been carrying it around for months inside the lining of my backpack. It was suddenly so clear to me what I needed to do. With that little velvet box in my hand, I was ready to go home and propose. No more custom bikes, or handmade knives. It was time to settle and make my move. I felt like the first prodigal monkey about to be shot into the grown-up space of kids, house payments and everything I'd tried to stay away from up until now.

Feeling euphoric, I wandered back towards the area where I had left the crew, down crowded streets, past tempura and grilled eel restaurants, until I found the boys. Ambu was sitting in front of the remains of one of his typical feeding frenzies—brown-sugar sweets, chilled cucumber skewers and *inago no tsukudani* (locusts preserved in soy sauce)—with sauce all over his chin.

Ambu is an Iban, a descendant of the headhunters who ran a major muck in their day, from possibly the darkest corner of the Malaysian jungle. Ambu is short, round and intensely funny. His frame disguises his power well. Ambu is strong and, given the right mindset, has no sense of fear. He wears the old-school bamboo tattoos of a 'headhunter' around his throat and speaks English like 'Tonto' from *The Lone Ranger*. 'Come we go,' he would say. I have known him for fifteen years, and he still surprises me. Sometimes I used to sit with Ambu and help him learn how to read and write English, and after a while he started reading everything aloud that he saw in English. 'Half-price specials,' he would suddenly stop and announce to the street. I told him I was going home to get married. 'OOOH, I come to your party,' he said, flashing me a huge grin and clapping.

Everyone had confirmed flights home except me, and the next day snow drifts and constant blizzard conditions made my exit difficult. I had made one of the most important decisions of my life while I was in Japan, only I couldn't get out of the country to do anything about it. I spent two nights in the transit hotel attached to the departure lounge at Narita International Airport waiting for a flight. Finally I was on my way to Singapore and then home, with no knives or bike parts this time, just a small box in my pocket that pressed against my thigh. It made me even more anxious to get home, back to Clare and the most life-changing exchange of words any couple can have. I kept checking the box in my pocket, just in case it had turned into a box of matches or a packet of mints—anything but an engagement ring. It was burning a hole through my leg. This is it, man, I'm going to get married. Christ, I hope she says yes. All kinds of elaborate plans for asking her the question were forming in my head, as romantic and surprising as I could muster without government backing and a helicopter.

I met Clare in a laundromat in Bondi. She was working there and I was going in with my offshore bag full of horrendously dirty rig gear every time I came home on crew change. This proved to be a little difficult when I realised that I only had that thirty-second window to ask her out. I mean, how do you do that? You're intensely attracted to the woman who's about to pull your manky, stained clothing out of an equally filthy rubber-lined giant grip bag that's been sealed tightly shut since you left the rig over twenty-four hours ago. Given all that's revolting about a working man's undies having time to develop a life of their own, I did struggle with how to attempt to ask her if she'd like to have a drink. Perhaps I should have gone out and bought a washing machine and done my own bloody laundry, waited a month so she had time to forget how repulsive it all was, then come back to ask her out. All that raced through my mind as she filled out the little receipt, hammered me with that fantastic smile and told me to come back at four. This went on for months. I ended up bringing in clean clothes, and then I asked her out.

'She's perfect,' I'd say to Erwin. We had been together for almost three years and I knew she was my future wife, but after years and years of listening to guys offshore talk about their upcoming divorces, and coming from an oilfield-broken home myself, I thought marriage was about as good an idea as Paris Hilton's hair extensions.

In Singapore, as I waited in line to enter the departure lounge, I checked the ring again. Then it was my turn to walk through the metal detector. It beeped. A pretty Singaporean girl with what looked like a TV remote on steroids motioned me over and waved her remote in ever-decreasing circles as the beep near my crotch got louder. I produced the box and she opened it, then shut it smartly and smiled at me in that knowing way.

I found myself grinning at strangers sitting opposite me in the departure lounge. They were filling out their arrival cards for Australian immigration. Occasionally, one would glance up the way you do when trying to remember your passport number without looking, and would accidentally make eye contact with me. I could see them thinking, 'Why is that man grinning? God, I hope he's not sitting next to me'.

As we boarded the plane, I was still checking my pocket. Yes, the ring's still there, not matches, ring. Every cliché ran through my head as I practised asking Clare to marry me. The flight was going to be a good one, it was only half full in economy and, being the 'red eye' departing at midnight, the aircraft was in darkness an hour after take-off, so I spread myself out over four seats and fell asleep easily under three blankets.

The main lights came on, burning through closed lids and waking everyone up. I sat up, the airline blanket crackling static electricity across my shoulders. They were serving breakfast, so I figured we must have been just a couple of hours from Sydney. My hand reached down looking for the box, but there was no box, no matches, no mints, just air.

FUCK! A jolt of panic shot through me. I frantically shook out the blankets, dived my hands between the four seats I had to myself, then I was on the floor. It's on this aircraft, I'm going to find it, I thought, as I squashed my head under my seat and groped around under the life jacket. Nothing but empty blankets and headset bags. I crossed the aisle on all fours into the gap between the seats next to me. A little girl watched my progress as her parents slowly woke up and rubbed their eyes. A man asleep on his three seats woke up when I banged my head on his tray table, sending a glass of orange juice into his sleeping face. 'Sorry.' He looked back bemused at the sight of a stressed bald man four inches from his face who had somehow appeared from under his tray table.

I backed up into the aisle and into a waiting flight attendant. She handed me a paper towel. 'Have you lost something, sir?' she asked as I wiped orange juice off the back of my head.

'Yes, a small jewellery box with a ring inside.' I stood up to a dozen staring passengers, all stuffing their faces with omelette and coffee; I was obviously providing more entertainment than the TV in the seat in front of them.

'As soon as we have finished the breakfast service, we will help you find your box, sir. Would you like some breakfast?'

I shook my head and sat down feeling shattered. She pushed the trolley past me and down the aisle. I felt like there was a black cloud forming over my head, the sense of loss growing in my gut like a chemical spill.

After a while I noticed the little girl was standing there next to me. She had a stuffed toy kangaroo dangling from one hand, and in the other was my box. She held out her hand, and I picked up the box and opened it—there was Clare's ring. A wave of relief crashed over me.

'Thank you, sweetheart,' I blubbered. I could have kissed her, but instead I got her a stuffed airplane from the in-flight duty-free magazine. Losing your engagement ring en route to a proposal is as naff as telling the teacher that the dog ate your homework, and I think that little girl knew it. All she did was look down and see a velvet box followed by a grown man on all fours.

Clare is, without question, the best part of getting home after a job. The look on her face when my key hits the lock keeps me smiling for days. It wasn't something I ever thought would be a permanent part of my life. Too often, the first victim of a life on the rigs is a relationship, but it was surprisingly easy to get used to the anticipation of seeing her after being away. This time I was bouncing off the walls with suppressed excitement and tension. I didn't sleep for three nights. I was so wired that one night at two in the morning I even got around to trying to assemble the Ikea furniture we'd stuffed in a cupboard months earlier, though it didn't take long before I realised that the multilingual instruction booklet alone would account for the entire Swedish suicide rate.

For me to ask Clare to be my wife involved getting into a mental state not unlike those karate guys before they headbutt a pile of bricks. Finally I abandoned my master plan and, just like everything else I've ever purposefully thought about in my life, I acted without the plan. I dumped the plan, fuck the plan, I can't wait, end of story.

It was early on a Friday morning. She had just stepped out of the shower and rounded the corner into our bedroom. I was waiting like a cartoon rabbit. You could have pumped my heart full of jet fuel and it wouldn't have beat any faster. You know those songs that stir up overwhelming feelings, there are one or two that without fail for a few seconds provoke your triggers to go off, and you're emotionally there, in that place, at that time, seeing that person, nostalgia like a tsunami covers your world, blanking out everything. And if you've had too much to drink when you hear it, especially if it's unplanned, you'll have to look away or leave the room, or smile like you're mental or cry. When Clare said 'yes' and I think about it, I get that feeling. Thank God she said yes.

When Clare said yes, in a sense it was like winning the spiritual and emotional lottery. It felt like it was a turning point in my future. For the first time in my life I had committed myself to something other than my own needs. I don't know if I deserve her love, but as the years go by I know Clare will always be there. Blind faith and complete trust work for me, life is just too bloody short.

We went to my favourite café in Sydney, Latteria. It's a great place, just a hole in the wall with wooden stools kerbside, and the best coffee and conversation of the day is had there. Our friends meet there in the mornings on their way to work, but on that particular morning I must have looked like I was sitting on the winning lotto numbers, I was bursting to tell them.

We started planning the wedding over the next six weeks, and everything was perfect. Then one morning I rolled over in bed, opened my eyes and there was Clare standing by the door with the kind of look that wakes you up in a second. Her hand was trembling as she held it up, a small white strip of card danced about in front of my face. 'Two stripes,' she said, her eyes wide open in shock. It took a full five seconds for the dustbin lid-sized penny to drop with a CLANG in my brain box.

I had a flashback. I remembered Drew, one of the first and best base managers I worked with. Not a big man, but in possession of a massive personality, Drew was the hinge pin into all the hilarity that threw fuel on the fire of creative pastimes in the Bruneian jungle. He was just fun to be around, and when there was nothing to do in the middle of monsoon season, and you were sitting in the staff house waiting for the weather to blow itself out, Drew was always able to think of something you actually wanted to do.

One of the guys had a massive one-hundred-and-fifty-pound Rottweiler called Summer who was playful, strong and dumb as a bag of hammers. At the far edge of the lagoon stood a cliff face, stretching up some fifty feet into the trees. During the monsoon it turned into a waterfall, transforming the lagoon into a river. Drew would wait until everyone was swimming about having a great time, then he'd climb around the back shallow side of the cliff to the top of the waterfall and sit in the hollowed-out rock at its edge. Summer would follow him because she was fixated on tennis balls and, of course, Drew would have made sure she saw him pop one in his pocket. Once settled in the curved rock right at the tip with a cold beer in his hand, the water cascading over him, he would show the soggy ball to Summer, sending her into a frenzy of excitement, then casually toss it over the edge.

The big dog would follow its flight path through the air, her tongue yo-yoing from the corner of her mouth, then with all she could muster she would jump into the abyss after it, treading air for a second then dropping. The guys swimming about below would get the plop of a tennis ball first, followed by the disturbing howl, before looking to see a one-hundred-and-fifty-pound out-of-control Rottweiler tumbling towards them. Summer loved it, but the plop of the tennis ball was to have the same effect on these guys as throwing a hand grenade into the pool.

Drew thought up another trip after that. Some of us had our dive tickets, so he rented a liveaboard dive boat and took us out into Malaysian waters to dive a wreck that was relatively new. We got to the right coordinates, set ourselves up and by mid-morning we were descending a rope towards the hulk of a cargo ship. It lay on the bottom in fairly shallow water at a peculiar angle, its bow pointing up towards the light. Drew entered first, through a missing window in the bridge. I followed. We secured a paracord line to a railing and descended a black corridor, our flashlights cutting through the water. Marine life had already taken hold of this vessel; instant reef followed by everything that lives off it had made this fallen beast their new home.

The odd fish twisted off, startled at our presence. I knew no-one lost their life when the ship went down so my fear was only based on getting lost or stuck somewhere and drowning. But the anticipation of exploring this wreck far overwhelmed my concern at the time. Curiosity would not get the better of me here, I thought. I started cracking glow sticks and dropping them like breadcrumbs to show us the way out.

This was only my second wreck dive, so I was still unused to diving within confined spaces. It's easy to become disoriented, which leads to the sort of confusion and panic that can kill a diver. The corridors we glided down gave way to more and more direction changes and stairwells cluttered with debris. I was fast approaching my bottom time limit, and we needed to turn back and start our assent with plenty of time and air for safety stops.

Drew pulled up near an open door. My torch lit up

his face, and he pointed first at his gauges and then up. I checked my air gauge; it was time to go—now.

On the way back he pulled up again, spun around and gave me an excited wave, pointing off to his right through another open doorway. Why, I thought, am I risking my life here? Then Drew pulled his bag open. We were looking for the captain's cabin, so we could take photos of each other on the toilet.

Later that night, standing on deck, Drew finished his whisky, leaned over the railing and stared into the sea. He was in his early forties then, and still vehemently single. 'You ever going to settle down, mate? Have a couple of kids and live in the burbs?' I asked.

He laughed. 'Maybe.' He had another plan forming in his head and spat a wad of chewing tobacco into the sea. 'Pauli, there are two things every man should hear in his lifetime: "I'm pregnant" and "We have the building surrounded".'

With Clare standing there, test strip in hand, those words lit up in my mind like a giant neon tribute to my idiotic youth. Right, that's one down, I thought, as I watched the realisation of pregnancy and an upcoming wedding creeping across her face.

My immediate reaction was joy: firstly, because after years of hammering my body I wasn't firing blanks; and secondly, I knew that Clare loved the idea of being a mother. I did a little dance and hugged her, although I was shitting myself inside.

'I hope my wedding dress will fit.' She sat on the edge of the bed and smiled.

Huge plans were underfoot. I sold one of my bikes, thinking of all the baby kit we would need. I lay awake at night staring at the ceiling, making lists and worrying about money. Now and again the debate and conversation in my head would get so loud I thought I'd woken up Clare, but it was just the sleep kick she does sometimes. 'Myoclonic jerk' is the medical term. As you fall asleep your brain interprets it as your body shutting down, so it sends out a signal to wake it up. I wrestled with my ghosts of responsibility night after night; great changes to my work life and home life were forming, as our baby was forming. I thought about it constantly, our DNA combining in a split second, a future human genetically preprogrammed in a few nanograms of matter, defined on a cellular level instantaneously, the miracle of life. But what will our offspring be like? I peeled the onion late at night. I think I was dealing with it like I would a new offshore campaign—you know, logistics, consumables, equipment, paperwork—assuming all along, of course, that I'm infallible, and that naturally our child would be too. I'd look at Clare's sleeping face next to me, her peaceful breathing, in time with chance rolling invisible waves through our curtain. Only months later did I understand how fragile it all was.

Our identities are the sum of our life experiences, and each of us processes our world according to our individual mind and the neurons therein. At the time all I could do was think about making that world as safe and happy for us as I could. I guess what we are never changes, but who we are never stops changing.

I'd look back at Clare and start all over again. I should have relaxed, I should have gone to sleep, but I couldn't because somewhere deep inside me I had to have a plan. It's funny, but now I'm more prepared to accept things on faith.

Our wedding was going to be simple, straightforward and uncomplicated, and right up to the big day itself, it was. Clare had managed to dye her hair pink; her scalp had reacted to the chemicals in the hair dye and she was forced to rinse her hair early. She was already worried about a hundred and one things that breezed by me like a Hare Krishna at the airport, but this new pink hairdo was the last straw and the tears finally welled up.

Normally I'm a proponent of telling the truth in these circumstances—'Do you think this bag goes with these shoes?' etc.—but having gained experience in dealing with a pregnant stressed-out partner, I say lie, lie until your pants are on fire. 'You look great, baby,' I beamed back at her. She saw through me in a second.

Erwin and his wife Lucy arrived the day before. Clare was dealing with her pink hair while sorting everything else out at the same time, all our friends and family chipped in, and the next thing I knew my wedding day had arrived and I didn't have a hangover from the night before.

It was early on Saturday morning, I was standing on my balcony drinking coffee and Erwin came out. 'Big day, buddy,' he grinned at me. 'You nervous?' Of course I bloody was.

'Let's go for a ride,' he suggested. So we split, tearing off down my street and waking everyone up. The sun was rising over the harbour as we skirted round Double Bay. Not much traffic yet, I opened up the throttle just a little, this day could not start any better. I'm going to marry the love of my life, my best man, in all respects, was right there on the machine next to me, even the air smelled sweeter. We rode on through the city, enjoying the space before the traffic descended into the morning gridlock. Erwin got pulled over by a cop, but in the spirit of the day he turned out to be more interested in the bike than how fast Erwin was going. Magic.

We returned home to an empty flat, and two suits laid out complete with pressed shirts. I quietly shaved and dressed. The boys would be here soon to pick us up. We were getting married in a beautiful garden only a few kilometres away, and by the time I got there everyone was arriving. I took my place under a tree with Erwin next to me. Then I saw her, walking with Philip, her father. She looked amazing, I was speechless.

The ceremony itself was simple and short. I looked around and saw all the people who have been there for Clare and me. Ruby, my closest friend, winked at me. This is it. Clare looked at me through her veil, I had never felt so happy.

Recalling your wedding is a lot like trying to remember a car accident: you remember specific moments with astonishing clarity, in slow motion, but other parts are just a blur. The reception is just a blur, but I can remember dancing badly, drinking too much scotch, and running away from Steve, who in a kind of bizarre tradition puts me in a headlock at every wedding I go to.

It started some sixteen years ago, when Steve was just a scrawny kid. I was good friends with his older sisters and went to school with his cousins. Every now and again I would put him in a headlock and sometimes slam his head into the fridge door. Steve grew up, and now he's bigger than me and much much stronger, and he likes to get his own back. I know at some point he will get that look in his eye, and when he does there's nothing I can do about it. He's done it to me at five weddings including his own.

At one wedding in a very posh restaurant, everyone was in tuxedos and gowns, standing around an elaborate bar that slipped out into a wonderful courtyard garden, sipping cocktails and making polite conversation, when Steve's switch got flipped by that last drink. He turned from the charming, charismatic man he can be into what can only be described as Big Foot in a suit. He came at me in that half-run, his tongue slightly protruding, shoulders forward, with that low, deep laugh. I saw movement from the corner of my eye and turned to look. Steve was sending wedding guests out of the way in a hurried scurry, their mouths agape. I smiled at the nice people I was talking to and asked the lady standing next to me if she wouldn't mind holding my drink. Then I took off through the garden with Steve chasing me. We ended up on the grass outside a big window, where people who had paid hundreds of dollars for their meal got a breathtaking panoramic view of two grown men rolling around on the lawn in tuxedos, one screaming while the other laughed and made grunting noises.

So there was Steve at my wedding doing that half-run with that laugh, that look in his eye. I tried to run but it was too late. You can't stop him, I've tried that before—everything from punching to kicking to smashing things over his head. I even stabbed him with a fork once, but it just makes him more determined.

The next day I woke up next to my wife. Clare was so happy. She was looking forward to the baby's arrival and talking about painting the spare room. I was set to go offshore in a few days so I decided when I got back to start preparing our home for our new arrival.

Three months later, Clare was doing well, she had

excellent test results and everything was on track. Then at the end of the third month we lost our chance to be parents. Sometimes life can only really begin with the knowledge of death, that it can all end, usually when you least want it to. Clare showed a strength of character that astounded me and made me proud beyond words. I had no idea how much power lies just beneath the surface of a woman's drive to motherhood. So for us, we will try again.

PHILIPPINES 2000
PHILIPPINES
IMMIGRATION
Date
Flight
Status
Stay

●折らないで下さい。
●カード②は出国時に入国審査官へ
* Please type or print
* Do not fold
* CARD (2) is to be submitted to the
at the time of your departure from

JUN 24 2000

PORTUGAL
GUARDA FISCAL
SERV. FRONTEIRAS
02 ABR 1978
ENTRADA
AEROPORTO FARO

PORTUGAL
09 ABR 1978
AEROPORTO FARO

ed Kingdom of Great Britain a
rt Passport

Visa ... pursuant to Memorandum
Order No. ... Permitted
6 JUL 1979
up to

Commissioner
Surname/Nom (1)
CARTER
Code of Issuing State/Code
GBR
Given names/Prénoms (2)
Chief, Dep. & Ent. Section
19
O.R. No.
726288
Nationality/Nationalité (3)
Date of birth/Date de naissance (4)
Sexe (6)
Place of birth/Lieu de naissance (7)
Date of issue/Date de délivrance (8)
Kabul International Airport
April 2006
ARRIVAL
JUL 2000
25

7 KABUL ON THIRTY ROUNDS A DAY

Everything in Afghanistan is the same shade of light brown, even the air.

Decades of war have left this once fertile jewel in central Asia with nothing . . . absolutely nothing. Bullets change governments faster than votes in Afghanistan, and that's why all the trees are gone, and along with them all the topsoil. Follow that up with seven years of drought and a population that dares not set foot in an open area for fear of stepping on a landmine, and you're left with air that's thick with dust and a frightening amount of faecal matter as open sewers run in all directions—I could feel 'Kabul belly' ready to leap out and strike me down at any moment.

My first glimpse of Afghanistan was through the dirty window of an old PIA A300. Impressive snow-capped mountains dropped fast into a giant dust-bowl shambles the size of Texas. The flight had been awful, though at least Pakistan International Airlines gave me a laugh when I picked up my ticket in Dubai. The airline's current advertising tag line, emblazoned on the front of my ticket, read, 'PIA: We're better than you think we are'.

Tom was sitting nearby, asleep. He's made this trip so many times it would take a man with a bomb strapped to his waist screaming 'Jihad, jihad!' to wake him up. Tom's a polite, quiet man who looks like he could be your local GP or plumber, but he is far from it. He is a PMC or private military contractor.

There are basically four types of expat in Afghanistan: those who are there to help, those who want to make lots of money, those who do both, and the rest who are there to fight. After twenty-five years of perpetual war the country's infrastructure is shattered, and as for the economy—well, what economy? Afghanistan is on aid, billions of dollars of aid, but because it's just so dangerous the work that is starting to slowly change Afghanistan for the better needs protecting. All those engineers, aid workers, medical staff—all of the people in Afghanistan who are from somewhere else—are relying on good security. Enter the world of the PMC. It's a growth business. These guys are former professional soldiers, using their skill sets and trade craft in this new booming private sector. And believe me, there's plenty of work.

Although most big oil companies will never admit it, they use PMCs all the time. I had been around these guys before on rigs in nasty parts of the world, but they were always too busy doing their jobs, and I was too busy doing mine. I had always wanted to write about them. My chance to embed myself with one such organisation and to quietly take a look at Afghanistan came in the form of Chris and Tom one rainy Saturday in Sydney three years ago. They were with a firm who was moving from land-based operations into offshore security work, and not just in far-off war-torn parts of the world. Just look at the amount of piracy in the Strait of Malacca just off Singapore, where there's a gun-related incident every day. With 70 per cent of our planet covered in water, you'd think there would be more protection out there, but no, piracy is becoming a common occurrence. Forget the romantic gloss made popular in films—good-looking roguish but lovable buccaneers just having a romp through your cargo hold. Modern piracy is cold-blooded murder.

I was involved in a brainstorming session on the potential threat faced by offshore drilling rigs, and lots of specialists were there. That's how I first met Tom and Chris. They talked about Iraq and Afghanistan, and for me the seed was sown. I wanted to understand what's happening there, why it was so important to the oil business, why guys on rigs all over the world are talking about it. I had a chance to see it first-hand, not as a writer or oilman, but simply as the grey man in the corner; all I had to do was follow Tom—he had the access after three years in the country. And now, after a long wait and a lot of meetings, here I was retrieving my bag from the carousel in Kabul Airport.

We walked straight through customs into the mostly empty arrival hall. The sun made me squint as we hit the steps outside. I glanced over to my right where eight large four-wheel drives were parked alongside a dozen heavily armed Westerners standing around looking as menacing as their automatic weapons, shaved heads, wraparound shades and goatees would allow—almost every expat is a former military been-there-done-that-kill-you-as-soon-as-look-at-you kind of chap.

'It's all about posture and appearance,' said Tom as we walked towards the carpark where his driver was waiting. Not having a gun in your hand here is a bit like going out and forgetting your belt. 'Holding your weapon a certain way can make all the difference to how the locals react to you. That goes for how you dress, how you look, it sends a certain signal.' Tom has been in the country long enough to know. He has experienced the best and worst Afghanistan has to offer, and in credit to his character maintains a smile and a positive presence that instantly puts me at ease.

For me, arriving in Afghanistan was a lot like arriving

in Sakhalin in Russia or Lagos in Nigeria, or a mixture of both; there were the same dodgy-looking heavy-set men loitering in corners with AKs slung across their chests, the same concrete meets fluorescent light strewn with bad plumbing, the same shitty roads. If you have a back problem, don't under any circumstances go on a driving holiday in Afghanistan; you'd be better off strapping yourself into a car seat and jumping off Everest.

We arrived at the Kabul InterContinental Hotel. It's not what you would think of normally when you hear the word 'Intercontinental'. This is not the sort of place with posh décor and uniformed bellboy waiting to take your bags to your plush room. However, it is one of the few buildings in this city that won't fall over if you piss on it. It sits on top of a hill with the Hindu Kush Mountains behind and a commanding view over the city spread out in front. My room was near the entrance on the second floor. It looked good for Kabul—that side of the building was obviously harder to hit with artillery. By the time I had relaxed and settled in, the first problem raised its ugly head. 'Oh no,' I wailed, and my hand shot to my belt as I scurried to the bathroom.

Twenty-four hours later I emerged ten pounds lighter and more dehydrated than a Kabul traffic cop. Just to be sure I would live, Chris and Tom drove me to the German Medical Diagnostic Center. The German doctor scrutinised my vaccination card, asked all the right questions, took blood, made me drink four litres of water, gave me the 'peel it, boil it, cook it or forget it' speech and set me free into the waiting city.

Surprisingly, there is a lot to do in Kabul other than get blown up and/or shot at. It has a golf course that contains real bunkers, a soulless zoo not worth visiting if you have any feelings for animals whatsoever, and a mine museum. I decided on the zoo. It has 116 unlucky inhabitants that are fed on handouts from Britain. In January 2002 the most revered resident of the zoo—Marjan the one-eyed lion—died. He had survived there for thirty-eight years through the Russian occupation, through countless rocket attacks, through the bitterly cold winters and dust-blown-faecal-matter stinking hot summers.

In the 1990s, when rival Afghan groups shelled the city into rubble, the zoo was on the front line. At one point a Taliban combatant scaled the wrong wall and ended up face to face with a waiting Marjan. The starving lion dispatched and ate the man. The following day the man's brother arrived, chasing revenge, and tried to frag Marjan by tossing a fragmentation grenade into his tiny enclosure. Marjan lost an eye and was lame for the rest of his life, but against the odds he survived. There are two new lions at the zoo now, 'Zing Zong' and 'Dolly', donated by China. I wish I could have paid my respects to Marjan though.

'Blitzkrieg' reigning supreme.

Blitzkrieg lying in wait … the owl never knew what hit him.

'Fantasy Island', Sakhalin, Russia 2006 ... spot the ex-con.

'No Fighting' sign.

A well test,
flaring in full swing.

Training centre with Calvin the ex-boxer; he can push his nose into his eye socket.

Erwin—not a rig in sight.

Dad in 1960; what goes up ...

El Adem, the Libyan desert, 1964.

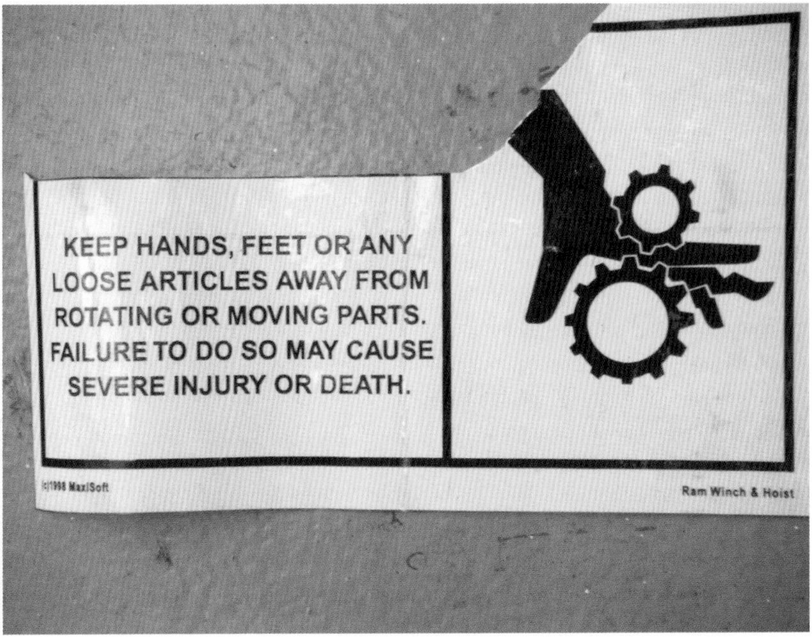

Death or even worse!

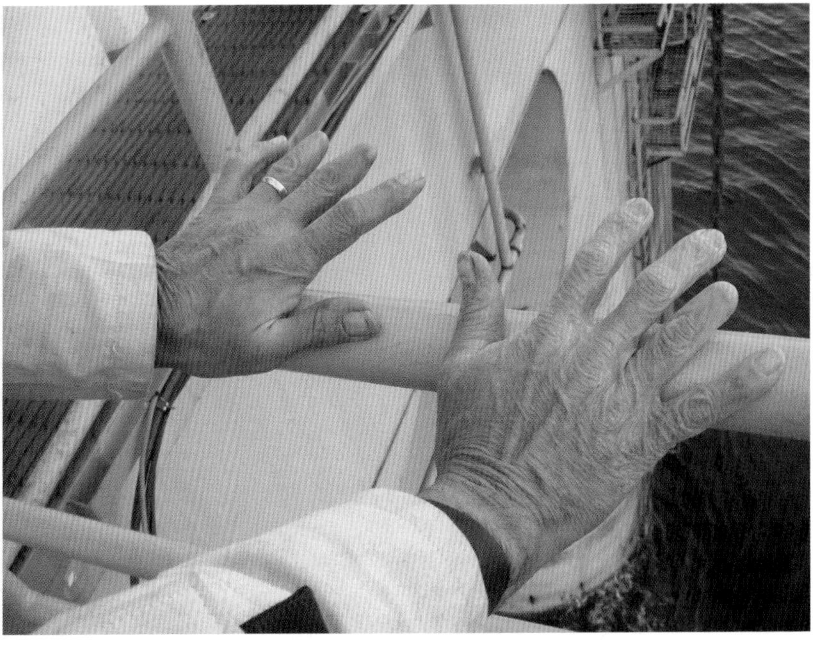

Thirty years' worth of damage to Bob the driller's hands.

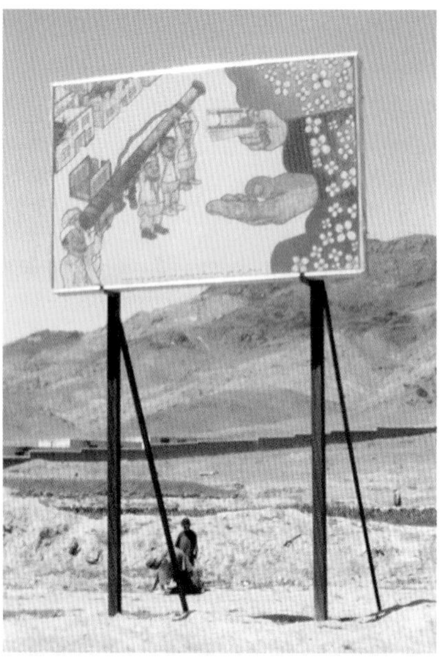

The billboard that says it all.

No room service, no minibar, no mint on the pillow.

How to buy your fuel in Kabul; make sure you pay before you pump.

Over ten million people live in a country the size of Texas.

One of Kabul's prettier boulevards.

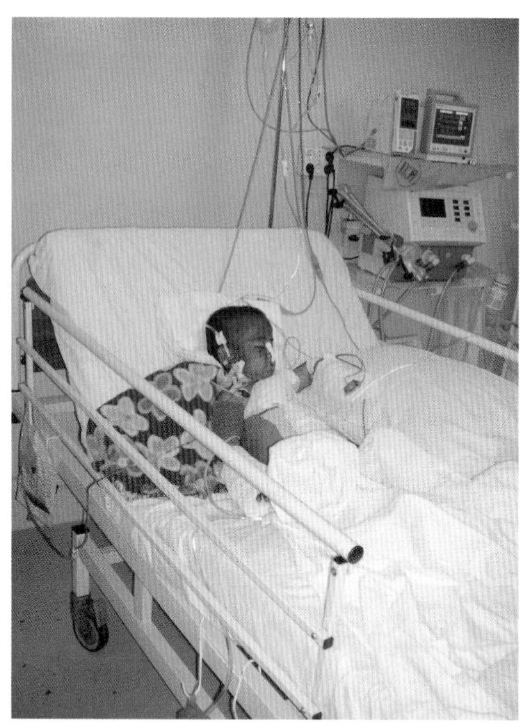

A little man in the fight for his life.

An opium field, Afghanistan.

Driving in Kabul was almost as depressing as visiting the zoo. Kabul's streets are packed with four million people struggling to get from A to B in a heaving mass of dust, shit (human and animal), exhaust, and entirely too many people with guns. The inevitable gridlock happens every day. As soon as the car stopped moving, the peddlers appeared through the smoke, much like they do in so many other countries. Over the years I've been talked into purchasing all kinds of crap I didn't need, by old women, kids and one-legged, one-eyed people whose final option is to try and eke out an existence by lane splitting in static traffic and selling everything from peanuts to guns.

Warfare has turned most of Kabul's former middle-class apartment buildings into weird shapes; most were bullet riddled to the point of producing a dimpled golf-ball effect in the concrete, with virtually every single square inch having sustained small arms fire. Others had 'surgically removed' balconies where RPGs and mortars had impacted.

This place put me slightly on edge. It was like Afghanistan was watching, watching and waiting like a wild animal, like a wounded, hardened, one-eyed lion. I knew I needed to treat it with respect, keep my actions introverted, my voice even and calm, and only show my teeth in a smile.

Tom was in the front passenger seat with his armalite, muzzle down, between his knees. I sat in the back, looking out into the dusty street. Each passing minute one foot of forward movement rolled by in an excruciating test of endurance. You're not going to get out and run, not in Kabul, so you may as well accept it, even it if means missing your flight, meeting, appointment, whatever. Through the hot dust a figure emerged, a boy around eight. He had big sad hazel eyes.

'Spandi,' said the driver and lowered his window. The boy walked over to our driver's door. I'd seen them on the street before in Kabul, these young kids, peddling tin cans of smoke like little chimneys. I had no idea what they were up to. They just arrived at your window enveloped in thick spicy blue clouds. The driver handed the boy ten Afghanis and let the smoke billow from the can into the car, then the window went back up and the boy was gone, on to the next car.

The cans, much like the children holding them, all look the same: charred, dirty and too fragile for their purpose. They hang awkwardly from rusted handles resembling old bent clothes hangers, and the smoke . . . what was with that smoke? I thought it might have been hash, tea or a funky decongestant. After half an hour of discussion with Ali, the driver, I discovered that it came from 'spand', a herb that can be found in markets across Afghanistan. One who sells spand is referred to as 'spandi' by the Afghans. When the herb is burned, the smoke produced is believed to ward off evil spirits and misfortune. The practice goes back centuries, buried deep in Afghan tribalism that revolved around animism and ancestor worship. The spandi eking out an existence on the streets are desperate, so they play on the superstitions deeply rooted in the collective psyche of the Afghan people.

There is a lack of basically everything in Afghanistan. The country is living on a meal ticket supplied by everyone else, and progress is about as fast as a tectonic plate. The 4.6 billion dollars it was promised by the international community has come up very short, thanks to a never-ending daisy chain of bureaucrats who pass paperwork around in a giant merry-go-round of red tape from one side of Kabul to the other. So what does it have apart from more dust than a British rail seat and a lot of poppies? Not much. Perhaps by some miracle in, say, thirty years it will have all the things we take for granted. Changes have been made for the better, compared to Afghanistan circa 2002, and there have been improvements in new construction, roads, power supply and medical aid, but by our standards it's still a mess.

Already two days had passed. I flopped down on my hotel bed, stared at the ceiling fan and let my brain go numb. And slept the heavy deep sleep you get after a long journey followed by Kabul belly and a nice day at the zoo.

It was lunchtime when I finally woke up. After a call to the boys and a quick bite to eat in the hotel, I was again stuck in Kabul traffic. Chris was next to me in the back, Sami behind the wheel and Tom in the front seat next to him. I could just make out a spandi working his way through the dust and exhaust fumes, down perpetually nervous and impoverished streets.

Sometimes we saw a car, usually military, with a big round disk on the roof. The disk is plugged into a bank of batteries in the back that provide the power for it to pulse out multiple signals to detonate any IEDs (improvised explosive devices) that may be buried in the road ahead. Once a disked car is spotted by the locals it creates a parting-of-the-sea effect, as no-one wants to be ahead of it if a bomb does go off—especially when the IEDs are becoming more and more advanced. Indeed, simple IEDs are giving way to what Tom calls 'off-route mines', devices that are hand-turned on a lathe, packed with explosives and capped with a concave steel or copper plate. The mine can be concealed and detonated horizontally or vertically, triggered by remote, infra-red or command wire. The explosion turns the concave plate into a molten jet or EFP (explosively formed projectile) moving at two thousand metres per second. It can penetrate up to ten centimetres of armour plating at one hundred metres. It creates a very effective killing ground and injects real fear as no-one is safe.

Suddenly the traffic started separating, everyone pulled onto the kerb in an effort to get out of the way, and a disked-up car ploughed past, leading a convoy of four vehicles at high speed through the city centre. The cars were big expensive four-wheel drives with blacked-out windows and armour plating. The spandi was caught in the mayhem of traffic, he dropped his can, for a second he was enveloped in a blue cloud, then in a blur the four cars sped past us. Every driver instantly tried to fill the hole the convoy had made in an effort to get an extra twenty yards down the street. Our driver did the same. I looked to my left just in time to see the boy; he was down, his burning spand smoking all around him. One of the convoy vehicles had driven over his left foot, smashing it to a pulp. He just sat there in shock. In seconds we were turning down a side street. I tried to get out, but it was too dangerous: the repercussions of the hit-and-run would soon send the people who saw it into a frenzy, and our driver wasn't stopping no matter what I did. Tom swivelled in the front seat, his face was blank. 'Can't stop, mate. You don't want to be there, it'll get nasty.'

Sami pointed the car down tiny parallel back streets, expertly navigating the maze laid out in his head. He is a former Mujahideen and has forgotten more about Kabul than any of us will ever know. I think my bum spent more time in the air than on the seat as we ploughed on, over small boulders and through potholes big enough to have a party in. My whole spine felt it, as any contact with the seat seemed to have the padding of Victoria Beckham.

Later that evening we set out into the city to relax and have a drink. My stomach was doing cartwheels again, thanks to the roads, but after a couple of tablets the German doc had given me I had regained control and was ready for 'Samarqand'.

'This place is the wild west, mate,' said Chris as we bounced down another Kabul back street. High walls topped with razor wire surrounded every structure, and there were big iron gates and armed guards who always made eye contact and tracked your uneven progression past their post. Tom was grinning in the front seat, but he was the one with the pistol on his hip and an M4 armalite in his hand. It was getting dark; random lights broke through the thick dust but visibility was no more than thirty feet.

'Put your game face on, mate,' said Chris as I jumped out of the big four-wheel drive and straight into a deep pothole full of grey sludge. The boys had a good laugh.

Luckily for me this bar didn't have a dress code rule regarding being covered in shit from the knees down.

I was asked for ID at the entrance. It's best to wear shirts and jackets with huge breast pockets here, as reaching inside your clothing tends to look a bit like you're going for your Magnum, and digging around in your pocket does tend to send armed men frantic even if the only thing you produce is a Mars Bar. I always give the doorman a massive tip when going into rough clubs in rough countries. I tell them if they see me running out pursued by some pissed-off punter, I'm the one they let back in.

When we walked in, it became apparent that if there was a rule it was that there were no rules. Everyone looked like an extra from *Gladiator*. All sorts of shady characters were hanging about, expatriates from all over the world, diplomats, UN staff, soldiers, ex-soldiers, spooks, dealers in opium, arms and worse. I fixed myself on a spot near the back with good access to the rear entrance and not too much light. Okay, I thought, I've been in places like this before. Don't make eye contact unless you're shaking some bastard's hand, don't bump into anyone, don't talk about the War on Terror, or 'OBL' as he was known, don't get drunk and, for fuck's sake, don't talk to any of the women.

Chris appeared with a round of beers, sat down next to me and rattled off the names and backgrounds of two-thirds of the men in the bar, every one sounding as disturbing as the last. Some were what the boys called 'Walters', short for Walter Mitty, meaning someone who talks it up; some were 'Bongos', or business-orientated NGOs, who were there for charitable reasons but got paid more than Somalia's national debt. The only attractive woman in the room was as popular as a naked prom queen handing out free beer at the footy; she was slowly backing away from a conversation with increasingly overt 'someone jump in and save me' looks to the room. The guy she was talking to had obviously changed from the dark handsome stranger to a fanatical big-mouth with a serious chip on his shoulder.

The bar started to fill with more and more guys: the full ensemble and cast of the ubiquitous 'don't ask me why I'm here' consultancy company. Some exchanged close quiet conversation, others roared in loud backslapping stories, chasing endless shooters with jugs of beer and cigars. It was a Thursday night, party night as the Islamic weekend is Friday, and by 10 p.m. it was packed, loud and everyone was having a good time. Then suddenly an explosive fight broke out. Two guys traded blows for a few seconds but were quickly separated. The fight was over the good-looking woman, who had, by all accounts, been with both of the men, and now hard stares across the room just didn't cut it anymore. So in the true tradition of drunks with guns, these two men decided to settle their dispute over the woman by stepping outside and having a good old-fashioned duel. You know, ten paces, turn and fire.

They dropped the mags from their pistols, leaving one round in the breech, re-holstered their weapons, stood back to back, swaying, then staggered apart; no-one was counting as everyone was either hiding or looking for cover. The younger of the two spun around, but in his rush he put his only bullet into the ground before his pistol had cleared the holster. Realising his predicament, he spun round the other way and took off down the street, zigzagging in all directions. While all this was going on the older and, as it turned out, more experienced of the two took his time and carefully aimed at his frantic, sprinting opponent, but missed. He actually looked genuinely disappointed and wandered back to the bar. The woman had gone; everyone just went back to their conversations, picking up right where they had left off.

Chris and Tom kept a low profile, and their people were also very quiet, blending into the walls so well they were almost forgotten. Most of them are ex-Gurkhas and can dissolve into an Afghan street remarkably well. The boys play their cards close to their chest, but it's obvious they are very good at what they do; even when they get drunk they remain aware of everything.

Everyone in Kabul can drink, and if you come here you'll want to, you'll need to. No-one here is without a horror story, and if you stay long enough you'll hear them all. The nightlife in Kabul is surprising. When everyone and his dog has a gun, and you never know what's going to happen next, it adds a certain moment of satisfaction to every meal you eat, every sip of whisky, every new day. The conversation is better, the jokes are fucking hilarious, and the drinks are never ending. For a moment it could have been another Kabul, the best version, the one from the 1960s, the halfway house in a righteous passage through a spectacular dope-filled wonderland en route to Kathmandu and enlightenment. One hit of edible opium goes for less than a dollar here, while I'm paying more than I do in Sydney to drink whisky. As far as good hash, opium and bad roads are concerned, Kabul has not changed that much since those halcyon days.

The drinks kept on coming, the night rolled into a full-blown drunk, it was spectacular and so was the hangover.

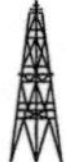

I woke up with a beauty the next morning. Chris and Tom were having breakfast in their office with a map laid out on the table.

'Morning,' Tom said and smiled the way you do when you know you stopped drinking early enough the night before.

My mouth felt like an Arab's sandal, but there was a lot to talk about; not the rosy-cheeked scamperings of the previous evening but about the following day's three-car convoy to 'Camp 87', a cement plant and road works eighty-seven kilometres from Kabul, past a few thousand landmines and other assorted unexploded ordnance, near the town of Gardez, right on the Peshawar–Pakistan border. It was a routine visit, so I jumped at the chance to go along and see the front line of Afghanistan's new infrastructure.

'Do you want a weapon?' asked Chris, rather like you would ask someone if they wanted an umbrella before a country walk. He knew I had used firearms before, but this time was different, I was here of my own volition and, more importantly, I was free to run away. 'It's like having a condom,' he went on. 'Better to have it and not need it, than need it and not have it.'

'No, mate, I'm not going to shoot some bastard,' I replied and gulped down my coffee. As much as I liked his analogy, I struggled with the mental picture of myself running to a twenty-four-hour chemist, as opposed to finding myself unarmed while someone empties an automatic weapon at me.

'Okay, there'll be plenty of support if something does happen.' Chris went on to describe our route and the day's events at a pace that was way too fast and detailed for my brain to retain. He showed me on two different maps at the same time, then suddenly stopped when he looked at me and realised that I'm no former fighter pilot like him, and given the amount of whisky I'd necked the night before he was talking to someone with the mental retention capacity of a wet piece of toilet paper. At one point, I think I may have even gone cross-eyed.

Tom sat at his desk reading something, then the phone rang, he answered and instantly sat forward with his free hand cupping his left ear. Chris stopped talking and we looked on, as the call was obviously not good news. Within moments I was sprinting down the hall trying to keep up with Tom, who was heading straight for the car, while Chris jumped on the phone. Tom relayed what had happened: one of his staff, an Afghan man who works for CTG, had been stabbed repeatedly outside his home in what appeared to be a random robbery. He was at the UN hospital and was waiting for transport to the bigger hospital.

The stark UN building seemed deserted except for the occasional small group of Afghan workers huddled in a corner and whispering together. Tom broke into a run, rounded the last few corners and burst into a room where Mr Nazari lay on a gurney, tears streaming down the sides of his hollow cheeks. Mr Nazari is a real person; he is a forty-five-year-old man, with a wife, a brother and no other family. He loves both his wife and his brother dearly. Mr Nazari could not understand the Spanish military doctors conversing with each other, but knew that his life was hanging in the balance. I stood unnoticed in the corner; the room was organised chaos. I could see Mr Nazari's eyes: he couldn't believe he was in this situation. He had lived through the jihad against the Soviets and he had survived the Taliban, only to get shived in his own front yard. He was aware that there were so many things he may never get to say, so many goodbyes.

The tears rolled down the side of his face and slowly over his ears. He looked around, slowly, his movement constrained by both an oxygen mask and a central line drip that was secured by a cannula inserted into his clavicle. He saw Tom, their eyes met, and there was a glimmer of recognition. Tom knelt down beside Mr Nazari and felt for a pulse. Mr Nazari mumbled something under the mask, Tom leaned in.

'Mr Tom, please find my wife and my brother, please,' he whispered. Tom's eyes said it all. A former captain in the British Parachute Regiment, he has seen men lose their life for cause and country but he wasn't going to let Mr Nazari go for this. The private exchange between the two men in front of me was intensely moving.

Mr Nazari was transferred into an ambulance. The arriving medics knew the prognosis wasn't good, they knew how much damage a human body can absorb. Just forty-eight hours ago they'd lost seventeen of their friends in a helicopter crash. The flags in the compound were still flying at half-mast.

The UN doctor was from Romania and the military doctors were Spanish. Together they went through the handover. One of the Spanish doctors directed the UN doctor's attention to the various entry wounds, and clinically cast aside the sheet under which Mr Nazari was lying, exposing his modesty. Mr Nazari was 'the patient', this was purely business for the doctors, but Mr Nazari was a devoutly Muslim man. Semiconscious, he tried to move the sheet to cover himself. He was aware of the Spanish nurse and was humiliated by his exposure. His movement was pathetic, there was no strength left in his arms and even less coordination. He continued to stare into the hard sun, his eyes never shifting, his pride never wavering once, his dignity eternal.

There are occasions in life to be amazed by the physical and mental courage of the human animal under stress. This was one of them. Later Tom would quietly relax, expressing himself with a kind of fatalistic humour and simplicity that both comforts and disarms. He leaves you with a warm heart in the end, perhaps because you know he doesn't really care what you think.

The next day we left the centre of Kabul and headed south-east. I was in the middle car with Chris and

Tom. No-one spoke, everyone was focused on the road ahead. Routine trip to Camp 87 or not, it was still a dangerous journey. Mr Nazari was still fresh in my mind so I paid close attention to Tom.

Wherever you want to go in Kabul, it's important to depart early in the morning. Those of us who complain about 'peak hour' have not seen Kabul traffic. There are no traffic lights. There are traffic cops, though, but don't pay any attention to them, as they are quite keen on waving you into the path of a semitrailer full of bridge parts.

The chaos and dense brown haze slowly gave way to clean crisp air. The new road we sped down cut a black line straight through the middle of massive snow-capped mountain ranges, leading us into the Panshir valley and on to Gardez. The predominant colour changed from light brown to green, and beautiful grassy hillsides lit up my window. Farmers dodged mines to plant opium, their land still pepperpotted by gun emplacements or the occasional howitzer or burned-out Russian tank with its turret still pointing towards a long-gone enemy. They were far too busy cultivating opium to fuck about with the remains of another foreign invader.

Twenty-eight of Afghanistan's thirty-two provinces cultivate massive amounts of opium—89 per cent of global production or more than four thousand metric tons that year. The farmers used to grow raisins, saffron and pomegranate for its oil, which was exported for use in the cosmetic industry, but there is too much money in drugs. Each province has a warlord, some of whom, I am told, are payrolled by the CIA as anti-Taliban allies. The regional warlords command militants numbering seven hundred thousand men.

Is anything going to change in Afghanistan? The Afghans are extremely long-suffering, which is why they've been able to survive so much. Perhaps that is why the country has not changed faster despite the foreign aid dollars. To the Afghan, we are just another occupying power. Having said that, the current, albeit undermined, Karzai Government appear to be giving Afghanistan a temporary artificial boost in development. But for how long? Compared to the stale developmental limbo it experienced under the Soviets in 1979–88, the minor development under the Afghan Communists in 1989–92, the fearsome civil war under the Mujahadeen in 1992–96, then the horrific oppression of the Taliban years 1996–2001, now it's new and improved, with minty fresh faecal matter and far too many guys with guns looking to make a fast dollar. Outside Kabul, Karzai is mercilessly nicknamed 'the mayor of Kabul'. He's trying to change the drug trade with the introduction of the 'Afghan Irradiation Force' who are 'fighting the drug war' in the provinces; that's a bit like trying to teach a monkey how to perform brain surgery with a pipe wrench.

But the Irradiation Force has been put to good use

on a few occasions. Such as when one farmer was having problems with his bull and couldn't plough his fields, so he placed an anonymous call to the Irradiation Force telling them the location of a huge, freshly sown crop. They arrived with brand new farming equipment and ploughed the shit out of everything in the area looking for opium seeds. So the new system of Western-style democracy has only brought an organised framework to old corruption. And besides, some say the biggest drug dealer in the country is the president's brother, with the second biggest being the deputy minister of the interior. It's just too big and too profitable to stop, no matter how benevolent the next dictator may be or how powerful the next liberating superpower is.

All this bounced about in my brain box as we bounced past the huge razor-wired gates of Camp 87.

'How was your run in?' asked Don Rector, the man in charge at 87, as he shook my hand.

'Just fine, Don,' I replied and smiled, trying not to notice the smorgasbord of weapons casually decorating his office.

'Hell, just last week someone took a shot at me.' He leaned back in his chair. 'Three rounds entered my vehicle from two shooters, one was on a rooftop, the other was dug in level with the road.'

Don is in his sixties and is probably fitter than me. He is tall, broad and looks every part the veteran he is. He has an impressive military background, and three sons all serving with US forces in other parts of the world. He explained how the system works. His company protects the guys who are rebuilding the roads. His men engage the Taliban in fire fights on average twice a week. They regularly find IEDs planted on or near the new roads. So in order to help Afghanistan's infrastructure take hold through new communications, roads, bridges and construction, you need all these guys with guns to stop the Taliban from killing all the engineers and workers who are building it all.

A metal bucket full of coiled up .50-calibre belt ammo sat by the door. I asked Don how often he uses it. 'Well, now and again they shoot at the camp, so I grab my bucket and head up to the roof,' he said casually. 'The fifty puts a stop to just about anything.'

'Oh right,' I smiled, thinking this man would be a pensioner at home.

He saw me eyeballing a bent RPG warhead sitting on the floor near my chair. 'Oh that reminds me, I must get rid of that.' He picked up the big green rocket and put it down on his desk.

The radio on Don's desk crackled to life and soon I was shaking his hand again, saying bye bye and hoping no-one was going to stitch up our unarmoured car on the way back to Kabul.

It's impossible not to be impressed by Afghanistan's rugged beauty, not to mention the Afghans themselves and their determination to get on with their lives despite their daily suffering and adversity, and what appears to be only the slimmest chance of finding peace. Ironically, this is one of their most enduring characteristics, as the Afghan culture reinforces the ideal of stoicism and obstinacy in the face of hardship. That must get frustrating for all these well-intentioned NGOs who want to help by implementing change.

The Panshir Valley is beautiful. The Soviets tried nine times to capture it, but it remained too strong. Now it's the one part of Afghanistan that has the glimmer of a new life shining in its mountain streams. There is food in the roadside market stalls, and the kids are wearing smiles as they tear arse up and down the road. Everywhere else ethnic conflicts flare up enough to keep people fearful and indoors.

The drive back was incident-free, apart from one road block where we had to stop as some rocks had fallen onto the road from an overhanging cliff. Everyone had their fingers on triggers and shifted nervously in their seats, scanning for a threat. I noticed a giant old billboard by the road. Left over from the Soviet occupation, it depicted two hands, one full of opium, the other full of money, and on the opposite side figures handing over a rocket. It was the international sign for 'We'll give you drugs and money for stinger missiles'. The stinger turned the tide of the war, and the Afghans shot down hundreds of Soviet Hind gunships with that simple shoulder-fired weapons system.

The boys dropped me off outside my hotel. I walked through the obligatory metal detector that beeped loudly. I have walked through metal detectors on my way through every door in the country. They almost always beep, but no-one cares; if the detector didn't beep, I'd be asked, 'Where's your firearm?' Back in my room I had a shower. I felt dirty, but still, the amount of brown muck that came off my body was surprising, as was the result of blowing my nose. I wrapped a towel round my waist and opened the balcony door.

It was already dark outside. Kabul lay directly below me, thousands of headlights and horns jostled through the dust in the fight to end another day. The bottle of Macallan on my desk looked at me and said 'I can read your mind', so I poured a big one, straight up, no ice, there wasn't any. The single malt bit into my mouth and I savoured the heat of its slide into my belly. The rich taste made me homesick. I picked up the phone to call Clare, but she was still at work. I looked at my watch; I'd usually be enjoying a whisky with my friends Sally and Simon in their nice happy safe Sydney garden. The gentle sound of small-arms fire broke my moment and slammed the reality of where I was back in my face like an angry slap.

I turned off the light and closed the curtains; it would be just my luck to catch a stray round while necking a scotch in my hotel room, especially after spending the day as a bullet magnet on the road to Gardez. The young spandi boy's face flashed into my mind. He was probably dead. It was obvious he'd suffered since birth. You recognise that unmistakable look, all of humanity's pain resides in that look.

It's hard sometimes to get to grips with what's happening here—is it just one giant power struggle to gain control of the region? Oil is the lifeblood of our modern world, and Afghanistan is becoming more and more important in the global struggle to get and move oil as we slowly, inevitably, and at any human or environmental cost, struggle to find more.

For now the only thing everyone appears to agree on is how bad the Taliban are. Sorry, I can't. It's just too hard to go through the huge pile of scribbled notes and things I've written on pizza box lids and cocktail napkins, hours of garbled recorded conversation with Afghans and expats who all end up sounding like Col Gaddafi on speed, just to punch out three quotes on what a sack of complete thundercunts the Taliban are.

In Afghanistan the war machine is stretched to its limit, like it is everywhere else in the Middle East. So the time will come when the job of soldiering is contracted out. It's happening now, soldiering to protect future oil, as well as liberating Afghans and Iraqis from tyranny—it's that simple. They call it 'security of supply'.

The numbers involved are mind-boggling; the United States has spent more than eighty-seven billion dollars conducting the war in Iraq alone, and probably the same amount on petrol, domestic beer and acne medication. Talk to the UN people and they will tell you that less than half that amount would provide clean water, good food, sanitation and education to every individual on the planet who needed it. Meanwhile we sit back in our new BMWs and wonder why there are terrorists.

Afghanistan could be more important to global oil supply than even Saudi Arabia. In 1997 BBC News reported that the American–Saudi oil consortium UNOCAL tried to negotiate pipeline deals through Afghanistan from the Caspian Sea. The Caspian Sea is a California-sized body of salt water—the world's largest landlocked body of water—that may sit on as much as two hundred billion barrels of oil, which would be 16 per cent of the Earth's potential currently estimated oil reserves. At today's prices, that could add up to three trillion dollars in oil.

As the world's quest for new oil reserves intensifies, so will the 'war on terror'. And the use of PMCs will only become more prolific as well. Guys just like me have been full-bore drilling for a century, but keeping up with the insatiable demand is daunting; current production (the number of barrels pumped per day, BPD) is falling each year, while in thirty years we will need more than twice the oil we need today. Imagine what it will be like in thirty years. 'Hell, I can remember when petrol was only two dollars a litre,' you will say. You might have faith, or belief in our system of government, or even lots of money, but everyone will feel it on every level—the end of affordable fuel brought about by our own belligerent superpowers and, of course, the inconvenience of upsetting everyone's weekend road trip plans in the West. But apart from that, it's all just fine . . . What time is the next appalling reality TV show on?

Afghan TV needs a show called 'Who Wants To Be a Normal Person?' followed by 'Survivor: Kabul', then another riveting re-run of 'Mass Murder She Wrote'. Can you imagine breakfast TV, with your appropriately jovial and upbeat presenters faking smiles and doing the daily 'faecal matter' count and car bomb traffic updates? Interviewing celebrity-obsessed Western visitors, and crossing to a guy who will show you how to disarm a landmine, and sell you today's special offer on the new 'Kevlar second chance' bulletproof vest. Just be one of the first ten callers and we'll throw in a prosthetic limb of your choice.

I had finished half the bottle, my head was swimming; it was like trying to understand free-to-air TV. The age of cheap oil is over; what we are doing is the long slide into post 'peak oil' propaganda. What kind of future will Clare and I leave for our children if we are lucky enough to have them? Within their lifetime it's possible they could slowly see the world end up in a kind of permanent energy crisis, a 'forever war'. If we're not careful, hydrocarbons and warfare will go hand in hand to define human life.

VISA
AFGHANISTAN
Place of Issue
Canberra
Valid from
15-Apr-2006
Valid until
14-Jul-2006
Duration of Stay
Thirty Days
No. of entry
One
Type of Visa
Tourist
Visa No.
1986/
Date of Issue
06-Apr-2006
Full Name
Paul Alexander CARTER
Gender
M
Date of birth
21-Apr-1969
Place of birth
Banbury
Nationality
British
Passport No
761019777
Accompanied by
xxxxxxxx

8 LEARN OR BURN

I woke to the sound of an argument in the corridor outside my room. I did the worst thing imaginable and had a cigarette, sat at the formica desk, turned on my laptop and listened to the argument escalate into a fight as my computer booted up. The perfect background music to try and make sense of this place. The phone rang; today I was going to the hospital. In order to see the result of warfare, the most obvious place to go to is the hospital. There is no darker place in Kabul than a trauma ward.

You might think it's strange that I would go to a Kabul hospital, or that the hospital would have the time to waste with someone who to all intents and purposes was 'visiting'. But, you see, as with all places around the world where conflict is tearing people apart and where there is a great deal of suffering, they welcome outsiders because they want you to witness what they are going through, they need you to witness what they are going through and to tell as many people as you can about it, because one more person knowing just might make a change for them. I was simply compelled to go.

'We'll be there in halfa,' said Tom. I put down the phone, showered, dressed and was side-stepping the 'What? No firearm?' metal detector half an hour later.

The main hospital in Kabul is operated by 'Emergency', an Italian organisation. The organisation has three hospitals in Afghanistan—in Kabul, Panshir and Lashkar Gah—as well as twenty-six clinics scattered throughout the country. On top of this, it also provides free healthcare to the three thousand-plus inmates of Kabul prison, and the orphanage where there are eight hundred kids aged from five to eighteen years old.

The building itself was a welcome change; as one would expect it was spotlessly clean and white, and within the walls in the centre was a beautiful garden with benches and rows of flowers. There to greet me was Dr Marco Garatti, an immediately likable man. He shook my hand and offered me tea. I could see he was tired and I asked if I should come back another day.

'Oh no, I'm fine,' he said, smiling. 'I was up all night in surgery, we had five patients come in, all with penetrating trauma.' He flopped down on a sofa next to his office. 'Just another day in Kabul,' he added, then scratched his greying beard and offered me a cookie.

Having already been in Kabul for two years with his wife, Dr Garatti was somehow managing to make a difference against a never-ending stream of civilian casualties, about 350 every month. He seemed to have an inexhaustible energy for his patients and staff. I felt guilty for using up his time, which would otherwise no doubt have been spent sleeping. He politely explained how much penetrating trauma is inflicted on his patients, from car accidents to mines and other unexploded ordnance. Three of the five individuals he and his staff spent the night trying to save were children who had triggered mines. On the road to Gardez the previous day we had driven past Kuchi farmers carefully ploughing in the hope that they didn't go bang. There are an estimated ten million mines buried under Afghan soil, and to my utter dismay fresh mines are still being buried by 'Area Commanders' (warlords) in the provinces. How does one hope to try and stop all this carnage?

Dr Garatti is superhumanly optimistic, and in his position I guess you have to be. 'I have six beds in "intensive care", and we try to keep a patient's stay in that bed down to three days,' he explained, frowning into his tea. 'In a Western hospital you would be there for as long as you needed, but here we have to try and move them back home. We train the family to take care of the patient, we have to because there is always another person who needs the bed.' He put his cup carefully back on the saucer, but the tea still spilled a little as his hand was shaking. He sat forward, rubbing his hands over his eyes.

I reached for my cigarettes in the silence, a knee-jerk reaction to feeling unable to say something positive. The packet was in my hand and Dr Garatti looked up. 'Oh, I'm sorry,' I apologised and put them away.

'By all means, let's go outside, I'll have one too,' he said and smiled.

I think short of jumping up on his coffee table and taking a crap, not much offends Dr Garatti. He produced his own smokes and we walked down through the centre of the courtyard garden. Here is a man who has devoted all his time and energy to saving lives that should never have been in jeopardy. His finger is stuck in the dyke, stopping the flow of blood from the Afghan soil. But he is under the gun.

Dr Garatti also has the only CT scanner in the country, so at any given time there is a mile-long queue at the front gates. On a daily basis, Pashtuns wait alongside Tajiks and Hazars for a consultation; everyone just sits down and quietly waits their turn. No-one gets turned away.

We walked back around to the main wards and I asked Dr Garatti if there was anything I could do. 'Follow me,' he said and took me into a 'clean room', where I put on a big blue coat and special covers over my boots. We walked through another white door into a ward full of children. Every one of them had stepped on a mine. Some were just toddlers, ripped apart but somehow alive. Three hundred and fifty children a month arrive here in pieces, and a quarter of Afghanistan's children die by the age of five. One little boy's face was completely unrecognisable as human; his eyes blankly stared through me. My heart fell into my boots, I could feel the blood drain from my face, my mouth went dry.

At the end of the ward there was a playroom filled with old wooden toys, half-deflated balls, and dolls also with missing limbs. Half a dozen children were there spending time with their parents. One toddler sat motionless next to a nurse. I watched him for a full five minutes. He just looked at the other kids playing and ignored the nurse's attempts to read him a story, although his gaze occasionally darted to the entrance. 'He's waiting for his mother to arrive,' the good doctor quietly explained. When his mother appeared through the door her eyes found her baby instantly. She dropped her basket, spilling fruit and precious milk across the floor, and ran to her little dismembered boy. The child launched himself from the chair and tried to run to his mother on what was left of his legs, then he suddenly floundered and ducked behind a chair. He pouted, angry with her for abandoning him. She stopped and fell on her knees, her arms open, her fingers trembling, tears streaming down her cheeks. The sheer force of her emotions almost sucked him across the room; he flew through the air into her arms, burst into tears and wrapped everything he had left around his mother. Safe in the warmth of her love, the familiarity of her hair and everything that makes a mother special. They sat there, oblivious, moulded together. Men with guns could not have separated them. I had to move away, as I realised I was crying.

We left the gut-wrenching children's ward and Dr Garatti introduced me to a boy on crutches. He was around twelve, his right foot had been blown off by a mine. The boy smiled and politely engaged us in conversation. His English was excellent. On a bench next to him sat his mother and sister. He was waiting for his prosthetic foot to arrive. I was amazed at how quickly he had already started to overcome his disability. He was just happy to be alive. With ten million mines littered around the country, it's inevitable that when kids are playing or just moving around they are going to set them off.

I had taken up enough of the doctor's time, and as we walked to the main entrance he put his hand on my shoulder and said that if I knew any doctors who had experience with 'penetrating trauma' and wanted more, I should direct them to 'Emergency'. 'The salary's not bad, and you would learn more in a week about gunshot and shrapnel cases than in a year in any major Western hospital. We also need anaesthetists, gynaecologists and midwives.' He beamed and shook my hand. Then another doctor came running up, his stethoscope swinging wildly. He rattled off a lot of high-speed Italian, and with that Dr Garatti was off, shouting 'Ciao' as he sprinted down the hall.

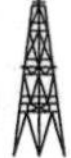

I wandered outside the hospital, rewinding the last few hours in my mind the way you do when you're walking out of the cinema. Did I just absorb all that? The street was full of people waiting to get into the hospital; clouds of dust kicked up by passing traffic had turned everyone into the same shade of light brown.

The car was waiting, but I wanted to take a bus. 'You what?' said Sami the driver.

'It's okay, Sami. I'll be fine.' I smiled, gave him my best 'I know exactly what I'm doing' look and walked across the road to the bus stop. The buses basically go from one side of town to the other, so all I had to do was get off near the centre and I could walk to the hotel.

Kabul has 108 public buses and more than four million people. Crowded does not begin to describe it. I waited for five minutes, long enough for the dust to paint me in the same way it had everyone else. At home where people are truly free, a crowd waiting for something will automatically form itself into a queue, a single line incorporating almost military precision where personal space is respected and no-one pushes. But in parts of the world where the people are mostly free only to get shot or blown up or run over, a line for anything is more like a mosh pit.

Then through a giant cloud of diesel fumes and brown air lumbered the bus, its brakes making the mosh pit cringe in unison. The driver pulled on a lever to manually open the door and gave me a blank surprised look. He said something to the man standing behind me. 'What the fuck is he doing here?' I presumed. The man smiled at me and moved forward, there was a brief debate between the driver, the man and everyone on the bus, with occasional hand gestures in my direction. As it turned out, the debate was over whether or not I should pay. Afghans, when they're not queuing, are gentle, generous people, and given the opportunity will extend every imaginable courtesy, including free bus rides for random bald foreign guys. I got on, nodding thank you to the packed bus's passengers, who all smiled and pointed towards the back of what looked like a dusty version of Dante's *Inferno*. There at the back in the middle was a free seat, next to an old man who was, remarkably, fast asleep.

After less than a kilometre I realised why the seat was free; the old bloke was letting go with the most horrendous farts. I nearly gagged. A pothole sent him careering into the roof. He landed back down on his seat, awake, but with his headgear pushed down over his nose. He rearranged his 'shamag', and in doing so retrieved a big fat joint, then he licked the end and winked at me. He's going to fire that up, I thought, and he did. By the time we were in the city centre, I was quite stoned from the various fumes he happily wafted around the bus. We had come to a grinding halt in the standard traffic-jam nightmare that is the centre of town.

A couple of passengers got off to grab a kebab from a roadside vendor who also sold bottled water and bags of mixed nuts. The more I inhaled my new pal's smoke, the more the water and mixed nuts caught my eye. Finally, after what seemed like an hour, I had the munchies. With a fist full of Afghanis that say in bold text across the top 'Da Afghanistan Bank', I walked towards the front of the bus to get off, but suddenly two men stood up and stopped me. It's unusual for Afghans to touch you, but these two guys were physically restraining me. Both were talking super-fast Dari, then one pointed outside and made throat-cutting gestures.

The penny finally dropped. It wasn't a place for someone like me to get out. I thanked them and went back to hide under my seat. After a few moments the bus started moving and I got up and shot a quick look out the back window, seeing what looked like six or seven cops in some kind of scuffle over an accident and some kind of protest march being led by the Kabul Municipal Post-Traumatic Stress Disorder Marching Band. To my surprise, Sami was following the bus; he saw me trying to look straight and grinned at me.

I spent the rest of the day taking out-of-focus photos in the highly depressing and totally deserted National Mine Museum. With the compassion of a cluster bomb, every device designed to maim and kill was laid out on tables. Perhaps I should have come here first; either way I was left with the same lingering hollow-fist-in-my-gut feeling.

I had a quiet simple meal in the hotel that night. I thought about the lucky ones who have no idea what they have, and struggled to fall asleep against my mind's need to unfold the day's events and somehow make sense of them. Feeling truly philosophical distended into myriad real and humbling emotions that in the end just made me angry. Tomorrow my alarm would go off at 4 a.m. Sleep eventually came through Kabul's confusing dust.

It was still black outside and surprisingly cold as I stood by the hotel entrance, rubbing the sleep and dust from my bloodshot eyes, my breath making clouds under the fluorescent lights. It was Anzac Day. The car pulled up, its windows clouded over. The boys were quiet as we made our way to camp 'Eggers', the US base located in the centre of town.

'Good morning, gentlemen. You're here for the service,' said the guard at the main entrance.

We were processed through and freely moved around within the walls. The service was about to start, so I found a spot off to the side and waited for the soldiers to parade.

The 'Last Post' hung in the air as the sun crept towards the top of camp Eggers's razor-wire fence. The thirty or so men and women from Australia, New Zealand and America's armed forces stood rigid in the morning light as flags snapped overhead. A small group of men stood motionless in the corner. Dressed in old fatigues, not showing any rank or unit, all sporting big bushy beards, they watched then quietly left. 'SF—Special Forces—guys,' Tom later explained.

Afterwards the Americans laid out a generous breakfast that included rum and coffee. I heard just how bad it was getting in Helmand, and more than one person advised me to stay in Kabul. I was told that within a week riots would break out in the city. This 'insurgency' is not a simple black-and-white struggle of fundamentalists versus foreigners. I had as many conversations with as many different people as I could. It was confusing, and even the name 'Taliban' may be misleading as it has now become a 'tag line' for a super-complex dynamic of narcotics, oil, corruption, tribalism, warlordism, PMCs, Arabs, Iranians, Chechens, NATO and, in the middle of it all, the West shovelling

Western precepts on a postmedieval economy. No-one knows what's going to happen, no-one ever will. The only certainty, as in life itself, is that people will die for all the wrong reasons.

Two days later I was at the airport. It's a lot easier to get into Afghanistan than get out, especially when the city is rioting. Getting through customs and immigration is like 250cc motorcycle racing: all knees and elbows. After a few well-placed dollars and weird hand signals to a man in uniform who held my passport upside down, Sami and Tom had me at the stairs to the departure hall. We said our goodbyes, short and sharp, the best way. The passengers nervously boarded as random people were pulled from the queue and questioned. I kept my head down and shuffled along, my eyes fixed on the first step of the boarding ladder to Clare and home.

Only after our aircraft was over water and descending into Dubai did I start to feel my shoulders relax. What did I learn from this? I sat there and let what I could replay in my head. I reminded myself of human dignity, resolve, compassion, fear, hope. Afghanistan reminded me that it changes you, more than you change it. It's sitting in freedom's nursery, but learning from all the bad kids. The man sitting next to me shifted in his seat and folded his newspaper; 'Kabulseye' said the headline.

IMMIGRATION AUSTRALIA
19 AUG 2005
DEPARTED
SYDNEY AIRPORT 3480
15 FEB 2006
PERMITTED TO ENTER AND REMAIN IN SINGAPORE FOR THIRTY DAYS FOR SOCIAL VISIT ONLY FROM DATE SHOWN ABOVE.
Type/Type
Code of Issuing State/Code de l'Etat émetteur
Surname/Nom (1)
CARTER
Given names/Prénoms (2)
Nationality/Nationalité (3)
BRITISH CITIZEN
Date of birth/Date de naissance (4)
Sex/Sexe (5)
Place of birth/Lieu de naissance (6)
Date of issue/Date de délivrance (7)
Date of expiry/Date d'expiration (8)
Authority/Autorité (9)
CARTER<<PAUL<
21 AUG 2005
19 AUG 2005

9 TURNING MARGARITAS INTO SWEAT

Coming home to Clare after Afghanistan I felt like the luckiest bastard in the world. Even packing my bags for the next gig in the Philippines, I felt lucky. That's what happens when you've been to the other side, to the places where you're lucky to make it to puberty.

We arrived in Manila without incident, the flight was great and so was the hotel. It was late so everyone just went to their rooms and hit the sack. The following morning we gathered in the lobby after breakfast, as our instructions had us checking in on a 7 a.m. chopper. Ambu had three croissants shoved in his shirt pockets and was slurping coffee while trying to read some businessman's newspaper without him noticing. I had phoned the rig at 6 a.m., they filled me in on the operation and, according to them, the weather was perfect for our scheduled flight offshore. It was a quarter to seven when the concierge came up and handed me a fax. I read it then turned to Ambu. 'Never mind that nice man's newspaper. Now's your chance, mate,' I said, handing him the fax. 'Aloud if you please.'

Ambu handed me his coffee, wiped the crumbs off his mouth and cleared his throat. 'Chopper cancel no go rig today,' he said and smiled.

There was a mixed reaction. 'Yes!' Don was happy. He was going back to bed so he could go out tonight and play; he has the sex drive of a gorilla in mating season. The others went back into the restaurant with Ambu. I sat down with them.

'Why's it cancelled?' Erwin asked me. I handed him the fax. 'Weather?' He looked out the window. 'It's perfect here. Did you phone the rig?'

'Yup, and it's perfect out there too.' I shrugged my shoulders and ordered coffee. It's like all things men plan when they're single. The plans are perpetually tentative because, no matter how big or serious the plan, if there's the slightest chance of getting laid, all bets are off. It's the unwritten rule between men and it's been that way since the dawn of time. If you hear, 'Nah, let's go for the summit tomorrow' or 'The launch has been delayed due to technical difficulties' or 'The captain has to turn back to port to take on more fuel', you know that's not really what's going on.

I was guessing that one of the pilots met someone on his way to the chopper. He was probably out there on the tarmac, with his sunglasses on, leaning against the cockpit, talking to her.

That night we all decided to go out with Don. He had been offshore for a few months on another job before this one, and it was his first break in what must have seemed like years so he was only interested in getting laid. As we walked into the 'Firehouse' he made a beeline straight for the toilets. I just parked myself at the bar, ordered a margarita jug, and waited for the dancing girls to slide down brass poles and land on a fire truck behind the bar, hence the name, and shake their moneymakers at me, small pleasures. For now they were playing some God-awful country song, you know, 'She peed on my carpet, She shot ma horse, She left me with nothing' and so on.

Don came out of the toilets with a lump in his pocket, sat down next to me, and eagerly rubbed his hands together while looking at the girls who had just descended the brass poles and started lip-syncing to a Madonna track.

'Why the dash to the toilet? Have you got the shits, mate?' I asked Don.

'Nah, I just took off my boxers—easy access.' He pointed at his crotch and winked at me.

'Oh Christ, put on a fuckin' rubber!' I handed him a margarita, but he was in a world of his own.

Don is my age, but he looks younger. He grew up in Texas, the son of a disturbed alcoholic father, and a mother who resorted to self-medicating with painkillers. That in turn transformed her into a reclusive shut-in, and as an only child he grew up fast. Don initially did very badly in school, the product of a desperately unhappy home. He was a loner labelled as stupid by the system, until his teachers gave him an IQ test as he was slated to be held back a year. That's when they discovered his triple-digit IQ, realised he was a fucking genius and put him in a school for gifted kids. Don excelled in chemistry, art and mathematics. He's a social chameleon, able to blend into any group and look like he was born there. He can go from brawling with wharfies in a harbour bar to attending a dinner party in town. I've sat there fascinated while he was being anecdotal and getting laid. Don is intelligent, resourceful and thoroughly ruthless. As an adult he is the one I have to watch, as Don could have done anything he wanted to in life. I think he's in oil because, on some base level, he likes the lifestyle. A global transient, he's independently wealthy, has no real fixed address and he's free of any ties to anyone—there is no surviving family, his father died in prison, his mother passed on back in the 1980s. He's moved in and out of places around the world on the back of our modern oil addiction, sometimes places sealed off to everyone. Don is fit and good-looking in an indifferent way. He can turn on the charm with anyone if he wants to, manipulating a situation as easily as you or I order a burger. Sometimes I think Don's a serial killer.

The rest of the crew wandered in over the next half-hour and we all sat at the bar, drinking margaritas and swapping stories. Don finally settled on one of the dancing girls and called over the mamma-san to talk price. She clapped her hands and pointed at Don's new girlfriend, who came down faking a smile at Don. She must have been half his size, poor girl; Don is a skip-the-foreplay kind of guy.

Twenty minutes later Don was back on the stool next to me. We all gave him a hard time but, hey, Don is single and in need of female company. Another half-hour went by, we were all enjoying ourselves, and a few other guys also waiting to go offshore came in and joined us. They had just flown in from other parts of the world so we asked them all the usual questions about what's going on with the well and who had done what to who and why. I noticed Don had been scratching his arse for a full ten minutes. 'Have you got fuckin' fleas, Don?' someone asked him.

He just smiled, but ten minutes after that Don's right hand was buried up to the third knuckle in his backside and he was scratching like an old dog. We were ignoring Don's mad fishing in the back of his pants when his new girlfriend came running up in her boob tube and high heels, the tassels stuck to her nipples propellering around in hypnotic circles.

'Honey, honey, I loose,' she said to Don.

We all stopped talking and looked at her. She held up her right hand; on the end of each finger was a huge talon-like false fingernail with glitter, palm trees and other assorted shit painted on it—except her middle finger, it was missing its fingernail. Don's face dropped in complete horror, he banged his glass down on the bar and bolted out the door.

'Oh fuck. Run, Don, run!' yelled John. 'Should I go with him?' he asked me.

'No.' I was laughing so much I could hardly speak.

Don's new girlfriend was already back on the fire truck waiting for another punter to ask her to poke her finger up his bum.

Three hours later Don came sheepishly back and sat down at the bar. He received a standing ovation. Don's new girlfriend was waving like a lottery winner at him from the fire truck. He pulled a small biohazard ziplock bag from his pocket and waved it at her, there was her bloody glitter-clad fingernail.

'I'm going to pin this to her fuckin' liver,' he said, grinning through clenched teeth.

'Now, now, Don, that's what you get for making that nice girl do sick things to your butt,' John said and slapped him on the back.

'How's that sock fetish going for you, dickhead?'

Don was ropeable. I was on the floor again, laughing so much my margarita was coming out my nose.

A few days later we were on the rig. The entire crew had heard about Don's new girlfriend and the poor guy was copping shit from everyone.

A month later our job was pretty much over, we were just starting the last section, and the crew had finished checking over our tools and equipment. I wandered up to the drill floor as I knew the driller on tower from Shell's 'Iron Duke' campaign years earlier. Mike had just come in on the afternoon chopper. I found him standing behind the brake. Like so many guys on rigs all over the world, we stood on the drill floor and played catch-up. I noticed Mike was limping a bit as he moved around. 'You got a parrot to go with that limp, Mike? What's up?'

'I got clipped by a drunk driver on my Harley,' he said. 'Motherfucker put me in a ditch and took off. I was in there for hours before someone found me. My leg was a mess, I woke up in the hospital and realised they had amputated it.'

I looked at him in disbelief. 'Come on . . .'

'No shit, check it out.' He pulled up the leg of his

coveralls and there was a metal shaft coming out of the top of his Red Wing boot.

'Oh fuck, Mike. I'm so sorry, mate,' I stammered, feeling awful.

'It's okay, bud, you weren't to know. The company really looked after me, paid for all of it.' He propped his leg up on the railing and pulled back his coveralls. 'It's titanium alloy, best you can get,' he said proudly and rapped his knuckles on the shiny tube. 'Eighteen thousand bucks.' It looked like it belonged on the side of a space shuttle.

Mike was a tough bugger. He had to learn how to walk again as well as dealing with the loss of his leg, and to his credit he was back at work six weeks after the accident. He poured a cup of coffee from a thermos and handed it to me.

'Cheers, Mike.' I was about to change the subject when Mike went on.

'So I'm all groggy after the op and the fuckin' surgeon is standing there. I thought my leg was still there, but when I looked down there was only one foot poking the sheet up.' Mike was telling me this rather like you would tell someone a joke. 'Then he says, "Would you like us to forward your leg on to your home address?" I'm laying in a fuckin' hospital bed in Singapore and this guy wants to know if I'd like my cremated leg sent to my mom's place in Canada. Jesus.'

There was a moment's silence as I was left speechless.

What do you say to a man who's lost a leg? Fortunately, Mike kept going.

'What's your problem tonight? Busting for a smoke, huh?' he asked and smiled slyly.

This particular rig had decided to ban smoking, and before we boarded the chopper to go offshore we were searched for 'any source of ignition'. They turned our bags inside out and removed all our cigarettes, lighters, matches, the lot. After a month I was starting to get more and more agitated.

'It's been a month, man,' I moaned. 'I should be over it by now, but I'm not.' I was biting my fingernails and eating too much, which made me feel bloated and added to my already wicked mood.

Mike wandered closer to me. 'Listen,' he whispered, leaning in, 'after your shift, come by my cabin and I'll get you a smoke.' I looked at him in confusion. 'Don't worry, it's cool,' he said and went back to work.

Later, after we finished at about two in the morning, I knocked on his cabin door, he answered and I stepped inside. 'Here,' he said and handed me a Styrofoam cup, a box of matches and a pack of French smokes. 'You wait till the guys in your cabin are eating, then get up on the top bunk, pile up the pillows, turn off the lights and slide the ceiling panel above your head over to one side, then sit on the pillows and stick your head up through the hole and light up.' I must have looked vacant. 'Are you getting all this?' Mike asked.

'Yeah, won't someone smell it?'

'Just blow your smoke into the air-con duct, put some water in the cup and ash into it, leave all of it up there, and just put the panel back when you're done. See ya.' He slammed the door.

And off I went to break the rules. Everyone was still in the TV room, so I went through Mike's routine, sitting on three pillows in the dark with a smoke dangling from my mouth while sliding the ceiling panel back and debating whether or not I should do this. I'll end up getting caught and I'll get run off—fired—and all because I can't go without a fuckin' cigarette.

When I stuck my head up through the hole and peered about, all I could see was a long line of glowing red smokes going as far as I could see in both directions; the whole rig was up there, all puffing away without a care in the world.

'Took you long enough, Pauli, you shithead,' Mike said from halfway down the line. Everyone burst out laughing, bastards.

The next night I was on the drill floor with Iron Mike. We were running pipe in the hole using a power tong, a kind of giant hydraulically powered wrench. It has two hoses plumbed into the back of a hydraulic motor, one hose being the supply line and the other the return line. When the tong is spinning pipe together, the volume of hydraulic oil circulating through the motor is considerable. It was while making up a joint of pipe that the motor seal blew on the tong, covering the drill floor in hot oil. I ran over to the power unit to shut it down while Mike sorted out the roughnecks to pick up the backup tong.

He came out from behind the drilling console and was walking over to me, no doubt to give me a hand, when he hit hot oil. Both legs shot out from under him, in that classic banana peel slip. We all watched as Mike's new eighteen thousand-dollar titanium alloy leg, as if in slow motion, flew through the air, did a nice little pirouette and bounced straight over the side. Mike had gone down hard, his hard-hat stopped him from knocking himself out, but he had seen his new leg disappear over the side. We all rushed over to help him.

'Get back!' he yelled, furious. 'Haven't you seen a fuckin' one-legged driller before?' Mike hopped over to the railing and peered into the night, his empty trouser leg flapping in the breeze. 'Motherfucker!' He was off, hopping down the stairs, to look for his leg.

The rest of us exchanged blank looks.

'Well, go and give him a hand,' I told Ambu, who grabbed a walkie-talkie and went after Mike.

After only a few moments Ambu was on the radio. 'Hello, I have Mike leg.' That was fast, I thought. The boys were crowded round the radio listening, and we could also hear Mike swearing below us. 'I come back drill floor now,' said Ambu.

'No, Ambu bring the leg to the galley, okay?' The

boys looked at me. I had an idea. 'I'm going to hide it,' I told them. There was a lot of laughing. 'Ambu, bring the leg to the galley.'

A long pause. 'Okay, come we go.'

Ambu was waiting for me with Mike's leg dangling over his shoulder. I had a quiet word with the camp boss who laughed when I told him I wanted to hide Mike's new leg in his freezer.

Poor Mike was distraught; he finished his shift on one leg and cursed all the way through his shower, his meal, the movie afterwards, and breakfast the next day. That's when we told him where his leg was. 'Bastards!' He threw a cup of coffee at me, and was off hopping towards the freezer. An hour later Mike was still not on the drill floor. I found him with a paint-stripper heat gun blowing hot air into his new leg. 'Can't get the motherfucker on, 'cos the cold contracted the metal, you fuck' and another cup of coffee was airborne.

That afternoon we touched down in bad weather at Manila's Ninoy Aquino Airport. The pilot shut down and we all hurried through the rain into the hanger to wait for the ground crew to bring in our bags.

'Just beat the weather,' the pilot said as he ran up to

us, shaking the rain off his head. 'I'd hate to get stuck in Busuanga.' Busuanga is one of the larger islands in the Philippines, where choppers refuel en route to the rig. It's a lush green paradise, though sparsely populated and therefore, I must admit, lacking in amusements.

'Why?' I asked. 'It's not so bad.'

'I've got a date tonight,' he beamed.

'Where did you meet her?' asked Erwin.

'Right here at the airport actually.'

Erwin looked at me, I started laughing.

'What?' The pilot looked annoyed.

The bad weather turned out to be the start of one of those Philippines typhoons that shuts off the power and transforms the streets into rivers. We ended up in a small bar that had this excellent seafood restaurant out the back and settled in for the rest of the night. It was pointless trying to leave; the whole place was in gridlock. It was close to midnight when the lights went out. We were the last group in there, all drunk, and the manager who had been sitting with us doing tequila shots staggered off to get some candles. Ambu continued eating.

'He's a machine,' said Erwin. 'Keep your hands away from his face when he's feeding.'

Ambu can see in the dark and poured himself another tequila. I was three feet from him and could only just make out what was going on. It must be one of his jungle skills or something, like his complete lack of fear. If Ambu is wearing his 'power belt' then, as he puts it, 'Ambu cannot die.' I've seen him work over guys twice his size. I've also read his medical file, or rather read it to him: the official diagnosis is abbreviated as NAFOD, meaning No Apparent Fear Of Death. To Ambu, the belt is his power. He believes in it and wears it everywhere. 'It's magic,' he says. Unfortunately, since airports have started dissecting us before a flight Ambu has been forced to take off his 'power belt'; he was causing small riots in the departure lounge when a security guy pulled a two-metre long leather belt, with human teeth and other assorted charms dangling off it, from inside his pants.

Jimmy, the restaurant manager, returned with a box of candles, a flashlight and a bottle of premium tequila. 'This is the best,' he said and went back to the bar for a tray of glasses.

'Keep away from children.' Ambu was reading the plastic bag the candles were in.

We had been doing shots all night—the salt, the sticky glass and a wedge of lemon pushed into gritted teeth. We did them all: the 'Body Slam', the 'Depth Charge', the painful and completely stupid 'Tequila Stuntman'. If memory serves, that's the one where you snort the salt, take the shot, squeeze the lemon in your eye, and eat the worm. A great many of us have spent the early hours of the morning projectile vomiting into a taxi while your mates remind you about the worm you ate after that last shot.

Tequila was never meant to be downed in one, with salt licked off various body parts, lemon was never part of the equation, and the worm was simply a marketing gimmick introduced in the early 1980s to sell more bottles to people who were so coked up they thought a preserved slug (that's got nothing to do with the drink whatsoever) was neat. Sipping it and enjoying the flavour, rather like one would savour a cognac, is the way to drink tequila. Mexicans drink it that way, or in the form of a margarita.

Still, we drink it, the new way or the old way, we will dance, laugh, throw up, fall over, but only ever on the surface. We all look after each other, even Don.

The bottle Jimmy was pouring was shaped like a big 'X' and it did taste great. 'Cheers!' he yelled and went off to get his guitar.

'Did you know tequila comes from the blue agave plant?' Erwin was holding his glass up to the candlelight.

'Yeah, it's a cactus.' I was really drunk.

'Not a cactus, buddy, but in fact a relative of the lily.' And he was off.

Erwin is a remarkable man. While the rest of us are telling fart jokes and chatting up the waitresses, he can focus and tell you something other than drivel. 'It takes roughly fifteen pounds of blue agave cores or "pinas" of the plant to produce one litre of tequila.'

Ambu stopped eating. 'Penis,' he said.

'No, *pinas*, Ambu. It's Spanish for pineapple.'

We then spent the next five minutes explaining to Ambu that the Spanish don't call the penis a pine-apple.

Don was dancing with his other new girlfriend behind the bar while Jimmy played his guitar. The others were either passed out or chatting at the bar. The storm outside raged on, the water slowly starting to lap at the front door.

Erwin went on. 'Tequila's origins are a combination of conquest and necessity, with mankind's need for war and getting hammered. Circa mid-sixteenth century, what you had were a bunch of Spanish conquistadors arriving in Mexico and running out of beer.' Erwin poured us another round. Ambu had finished his fifth crab and settled in for what was to be his bedtime story. 'Having an intimate knowledge of the distillation process as well as warfare proved useful in between brawls in the sleepy town of Tequila. They discovered after long chats with the locals that the blue agave produced a sweet sap that, once fermented, was a knockout beverage. The native Indians had been drinking it for nine thousand years, but once the conquistadors had finished with it, the fun really started, and there you have it. "Tequila" the town had produced "tequila" the drink. Tequila is also the name of the volcano overlooking the town and probably the name of the dog that lived in the pub where it was first poured.' He sat back smiling, Ambu had started snoring.

'This is so much better than the crap we've been drinking all night,' I said.

'That's why I didn't join in.' Erwin had been on light beer up until then. 'Understanding the difference between the two can get complicated, so first, in case you were wondering, there is no "mescaline" in mescal. The word "mescal" is often used with tequila as roughly translated it means "cheers". It's part of Mexican culture, a social icon, simply a toast as well as a drink. The best way of describing the two is to say that they are made from different types of agave plant and different amounts of sugars.' He leaned in and pointed at his glass. 'They are distilled in different ways, but to put it bluntly it can be likened to the difference between single malt, and rye or sour mash whiskies, or if you prefer cognac and brandy. I love this one.'

The difference between Erwin and Don, I thought, is much the same. I looked over at the bar where Don was licking his tequila off his other new girlfriend's thigh while Erwin sipped his in the corner and laughed. Erwin is the boss, his depths are a complete mystery, but he can handle the roughest crews with a skill I could never match, even when they get really wild, close the doors of the bar, turn the plane upside down and cut their toes off.

At some point Don was in the kitchen helping Jimmy with the crabs for the next day, when he got the idea to have crab races down the hall between the bar and the restaurant.

'Sheeet son, this'll be fun,' he beamed. The crabs were massive, each had a body the size of a frisbee. Their huge claws were tied up with string, but their legs were going like the clappers.

'C'mon, I've got the three biggest ones in the sink.' Don was leaning on his other new girlfriend who looked suspiciously like a man.

We taped different coasters to the back of the three crabs and set them up in the hallway. Erwin, Don, Ambu, Jake, John, the waitress and Don's other new girlfriend all sat on the floor on cushions, their backs leaning against the far wall with their legs stretched out under a big glass coffee table where the drinks sat. I was up the other end of the hall with Jimmy, who giggled so much he nearly fell over trying to control three pissed-off giant mud crabs. Jimmy had pulled out three drawers from a wooden desk in his office and we had a crab under each upturned drawer. They were so strong that if you stopped holding the drawer it would take off down the hall.

'Okay, you ready?' Jimmy was all set. 'On three.' I struggled with the drawers. 'One, two three!' We flipped up the drawers and the crabs bolted. Team 'San Miguel' climbed over the drawer and straight onto my foot, then back into the kitchen. The other two were neck and neck down the hall, going straight for the coffee table. Ambu was waving his arms and slapping his thigh like people do at horse races. Don's crab, Team 'Heineken', crossed the line first. His other new girlfriend rolled over onto his lap and kissed him.

The race over, Ambu and John went after the second crab, who had made a break for the door, while Jimmy was in the kitchen putting 'San Miguel' back in the crate. Don's winning crab was under the coffee table with Don's bare feet.

'Okay, who's drinking?' He suddenly stopped, his eyes locked on his other new girlfriend's—they may have been separated by countless cultural and socioeconomic barriers, but the look on Don's face crossed them all instantly. I'd never had a small Asian woman fired across a table at me before.

There was the most blood-curdling scream. The crab, with the bigger of its claws free of the string, had latched onto Don's little toe and, being not too happy with the whole crab-racing thing, it had decided to cut off Don's toe altogether. Don kicked over the glass coffee table, smashing it to pieces, grabbed a huge round glass ashtray and beat the crab into pulp, while his other new girlfriend screamed and ran on the spot with one high heel on. By the time Don finished, the claw was the only thing left; still attached to Don's toe, it lay there among all the broken glass. The place looked like a Tom Waits song. Don refused to go to the hospital. Besides, in our state we wouldn't have made it to the end of the street. Eventually, he opted instead to cremate his toe on Jimmy's barbeque.

IMMBRUIMMBRUIMMBRUIMMBRUIMM

BRUNEI DARUSSALAM

****

ENTRY VISA

Visa no : KB/52717

Reference no : KB/67

Category: ~~Single entry~~/multiple entries to Brunei Darussalam not later than 17. 5. 2000 provided this passport remains valid.

For Controller of Immigration
Brunei Darussalam

Date 17 MAY 1999

Fee: $ 30/- Rt. no: 4

VS 02

MALAYSIA IMMIGRATION
SG. TUJUH, SARAWAK
SOCIAL/BUSINESS VISIT PASS
Reg. 11, Imm. Regs. 63

AUSTRALIA RESIDENT VISA

No. 3222 57715X

This Visa does not authorise entry to Australia. ENTRY is subject to the grant of an ENTRY PERMIT on arrival.

EDINBURGH

Valid for ONE journeys by the Holder BEFORE OCT 1985

INTERNATIONAL AIRPORT

10 HURRY UP AND WAIT

Three months after Clare and I were married, we finally got around to our honeymoon. I had six weeks off so we went to visit Europe and my family, and hopefully not get into any trouble. It made a nice change when we got to the red line at the airport. I hate the red line. Usually Clare stands right on it, we go through our goodbyes, I would cross it, walk a few yards, stop just before the barrier where immigration starts, and look back. Clare would still be standing on the red line, waving, tears rolling down her cheeks. We had done that so many times, but not this time. This time she was crossing the red line with me.

Airports throughout the Western world are, I think, designed by the same firm. Each is just a slight variation on a theme. If you get hungry after you have gone through immigration, you get nailed twenty dollars for a very average cup of coffee and a bun. It's like you're in a limbo state, temporarily a citizen of no country, you're in airport land where they can charge whatever they want.

The good ones give you a trolley for free, like Singapore's Changi Airport, but in most of them you have to pay. Why? They make so much money, why do they think they can get away with stitching you up two dollars for their crappy little trolley? This is especially annoying when you discover, after arriving in a foreign land, that the machine dispensing the trolleys only accepts local coins. Japanese trolleys are free and by far the best ones I've used; they have a flip-up bar at the front that springs up as you pull the trolley out and stops your bags from falling off, and they have brakes, suspension and no mind of their own. British ones also have brakes, and a sticker on the lever that tells you to apply the brakes on a gradient. However, every time I'm at Heathrow I witness a hilarious trolley prang, usually involving an elderly person who has suddenly lost control of their trolley on a slope and embarked on a slalom down towards some unlucky punter coming the other way.

So Clare and I crossed the red line together, went through the current improved security check—screen, pat-down, sniff test, strip-search—and wandered into the labyrinth that is an international airport departure building. This one is like a shrine to last-minute consumerism, another award-winning design by architects 'Can We Cheat 'Em, and How'. It could fit like Lego into any other airport terminal in the world. While Clare went off to arm herself with magazines, I found a spot in the corner and sat quietly watching. The airport is a good place to observe the human animal under stress. Travellers scampered in that hurried way like migrating hedgehogs across a busy road. Backpackers walked past, almost floating after having checked in their massive backpacks that always look like they weigh twice as much as the owner, who has to lie down to get the pack on, only to realise they can't get back up. Tourists in 'Bondi' T-shirts were going home after getting various degrees of skin cancer.

For once, I wasn't dreading the flight. We were flying business class; I have done my time in economy. The airlines discovered ages ago that they can physically cram an adult human into a space barely comfortable for a chimp as long as they tell you beforehand that you may lose all feeling in your extremities after the first hour. This could be permanent, and if you're unfit, diabetic, fat, a smoker or just unlucky it could lead to deep vein thrombosis and kill you, but only after you're enjoying your first day on the beach. For me, there would be no elbow brawls over the armrest, no fake smiles from cabin attendants whose teeth are so bright that I need sunglasses just to look at them, no mini-meals with a metal fork and a plastic knife, or some crappy pre-made cheese sandwich getting dumped on my tray table for $12.98. Instead our flight was remarkably nice; we had a whole human-sized seat each.

Sixteen hours later we landed in Paris. During the hour we waited for our luggage to appear I went off to get a trolley. The French trolleys are free but look like reject designs for a light aircraft undercarriage, they career off in random directions much like the supermarket ones do, and they always seem to have one wheel that appears to be having a fit of some kind.

We had a fantastic ten days in France. We visited my mum and John, her second husband and an all-round legend. They threw a party, inviting their friends. Sitting down to eat with a dozen retired people, I was surprised to find that they knew how to party. It was like being at a 'Bond Villain' convention.

Afterwards we went up to Scotland to visit Klaas, an oilfield mate who was the company man on my first job offshore. He was with Shell and I was there to learn how to inspect pipe. Klaas saw his opportunity to completely mess up my head. He called me into his office. Erwin was there too, keeping a straight face. I had been working for a full day and all night, trying to make a good impression, but in the early hours of the morning Erwin had come out on deck and told me to go to bed. I wasn't working for him yet, I was with another outfit who had sent me out there on my own. Erwin certainly didn't need to take over from me, but he did anyway, and did a better job in the end. Mid-morning, I had just woken up and was standing in the company man's office. 'So, Paul,' said Klaas, 'did you inspect our pipe last night?'

If he knew Erwin had done half the work then I was in big trouble. 'Well, Mr Van der Plaas, you see, I was getting tired, and Erwin here was nice enough to take over for me . . .'

He cut in, 'Does Erwin have the right pipe inspector's tickets?'

I looked at Erwin, who shrugged at me.

'He doesn't even work for the same company as you.' Klass looked really serious. 'Take a seat,' he said and nodded towards a chair in the corner. I sat down. I'm going to get run off, I thought.

Klaas picked up the phone on his desk and began banging his index finger down on the buttons while he glared at me through the smoke rising from the Marlboro dangling from his bottom lip. Erwin just sat there, pulling all the right faces. I was shitting myself.

Klass suddenly launched into a high-speed Dutch conversation. Occasionally I heard my name, some bad language, my name again, oh God, now the company name; he looked at his watch, glared at me again, then he was talking about choppers. That's it, I thought, he's got me on the next chopper, the end of the shortest oilfield career in history. He banged down the phone, leaned back in his chair, had a long drag on his smoke and exhaled, his eyes hard and fixed.

I was waiting for it, indeed now fully expecting it. He sat forward in his big company man's chair and started laughing. Erwin jumped up and was out the door, laughing all the way down the hall. 'Ya, it's okay buddy, we're just fucking with you. Go and get some sleep.'

I got up and turned to go, then stopped and asked, 'Who did you call?'

Klaas was still laughing. 'My wife. I just bullshitted about who's out here, and what she's cooking for dinner tonight.'

Fifteen years later and he's not changed a bit. Klaas is bright and has done well in his career. I went to a work function with him and ended up sitting next to some ambassador's wife making polite conversation while Klaas pulled faces across the table at me.

The next day I ran into another guy, at Aberdeen Airport. I was leaving for London, walking towards departures. He had just arrived from a rig and was walking towards arrivals. We approached each other, glanced, made eye contact for a second, then continued on our paths. Then we both stopped about three meters apart and turned around at the same time.

It was Donald, I hadn't seen him in years. When I knew him, he was a driller. Now he was a company man; everyone has moved on, done well and become successful in oil, except me. I'm still doing the same shit I was doing ten years ago. But he was just as I remembered him, and within five minutes we had abandoned our respective plans and were sitting in the airport bar.

The last time I saw Donald, he was getting fired. A new tool pusher had come out to our rig in a quiet corner of the South China Sea and took a disliking to Donald. This escalated over the next few weeks, culminating in an explosive display of what happens when you wind up Donald. All I remember was the tool pusher getting punched, falling over and Donald casually picking him up by his ankles and dangling him over the side of the drill floor. The guy was beside himself, screaming while the contents of his pockets spiralled down to the sea some two hundred feet below. Donald eventually put him down and walked off to the locker room, as he knew the chopper would be en route within the hour.

That's one of the things that never ceases to amaze me about the oilfield: you could be sitting in some God-awful backwater on your way to or coming from a job and run into someone you worked with years ago, and you pick up right where you left off. If it doesn't happen that way, then it will on the job. Once I was standing on the drill floor on a jack-up rig in Asia, sucking on a boiled sweet and thinking about a workover job we were about to start, when a Baker fishing-hand marched up to me. Fishing-hands are specialists, like directional drillers who speak their own dialect that revolves around the language of drilling. They retrieve lost 'items' from a well. They are skilled individuals who use various 'fishing tools' down an open or cased hole, and they can fish everything out from a drill pipe to hand tools or the occasional unlucky roughneck, but that could be a myth. He was older than me by about twenty years, and had strong features and a purposeful stride. He took off his safety glasses when he was standing right in front of me, gave me a hard look and said, 'Spit that shit out, Paul. If your mother saw that, she would kick your arse.'

I was completely bamboozled and quickly looked around. Is this guy mental? I thought. So I cupped my gloved hand under my chin and spat out my sweet, totally taken aback and a little worried about what this guy's problem was.

'Oh shit. Sorry, mate, I thought you were chewing tobacco.' He gave me a huge grin, he could see that I had no idea who he was. 'It's me, you fuckwit, Tony.'

I was blank.

'Tony Lacey. Shit, you used to play with my kids, come over for barbeques.'

Finally I remembered. My parents worked with Tony when I was eight, but to him it may have well been yesterday. He recognised me straightaway. That's the oilfield.

Clare had to go home a few days before me for work. I didn't want her to go; I didn't want our trip to end. When my turn came, things got complicated, they always do. I departed London on the seventh of the seventh; exactly one year since I'd arrived in the middle of the bombings. The city was functioning as it normally would, but there were masses of people attending memorial services at tube stations, flowers and wreaths adorned station entrances, and all over London crowds had gathered. I took a cab to Paddington Train Station where I planned to catch the Heathrow Express to the airport. The cab ride seemed to take forever, and when I did get to Paddington I emerged from the cab into a sea of people. It was peak hour times ten, I've never seen so many people. The central staircase descending to the tube was a river of people. Moving against the flow was impossible; it was like trying to move through a packed nightclub, with luggage. I stood there for a moment, just looking into the void, then picked up my offshore bag and ran the gauntlet over to a café on my left. It was strangely unoccupied, so I ordered coffee and parked my arse in the corner, deciding to kill the next hour there before braving the hordes. There was an air of worry and concern in every face that went past, the horror twelve months ago still alive in their memories.

I pulled a magazine I'd nicked from the hotel lobby coffee table out of my bag and settled in, blanking out the millions around me. It was one of those blokey mags with a model in a bikini holding an automatic weapon on the cover. After forty pages of beer, sport and tits, followed by a sudoku puzzle, I was successfully distracted enough to relax.

That's when I noticed the black Samsonite suitcase under the table next to me.

It was one of those smaller ones that you can bring into the aircraft as hand luggage. The masses flowed past, ignoring the empty café and its unattended bag, as did the guy running the place. I sat there for a moment, then called him over and asked for a latte. 'Whose case is that mate?' I pointed at the suitcase.

He bent down to look. 'I have no idea,' he replied, and instinctively and cleverly backed away towards the shelter of his cardboard booth.

I got up and walked the few metres to his booth. 'Look, make my coffee and I'll be back with a security guy, okay?' He just nodded, keeping his eyes on the suitcase.

I picked up my offshore grip bag and stood on a chair. Throughout the tube stations and train stations in London there were posters to recruit new security staff, in a push to put people at ease. These new staff wear a luminous yellow vest and carry a two-way radio, but spotting one was proving difficult. Then I saw one, with his back to me, also trying to stay out of the flow of people. He was too far away to hear me, so I waded in. At first I was carried along with the current of people; no-one gives a fuck or gets out of your way so you have to just go head down and barge. Finally I got to him and explained that I'd found an unattended bag. He got on the radio, then said, 'Show me.'

The café now had a German family sitting at my table. They were oblivious to the suitcase, and the dad had also become fascinated in the beer steins, guns and airbrushed topless cheerleaders. The café guy was still in his booth with my coffee sitting on the counter in front of him.

I pointed at the suitcase. 'There it is.' I went to the booth to pay for my coffee, and by the time I'd turned around the German father was gathering up his children, one under each arm, and jumping into the mad faceless blur of people flowing past the café's boundary, his wife, struggling with the luggage, swept along behind him, their steaming drinks all sitting on the table untouched.

The security guy was back on his radio. I stood at the booth with the café guy and watched two more security guys roll up through the masses. One walked over to us. 'No idea who left it, mate?' he asked the café guy, who shook his head and began to look worried.

The suitcase was nameless; it sat there looking more and more conspicuous. Two of the security guys very carefully lifted up the table that the suitcase sat under and moved it away. Then they all stood around it and talked. Finally, one leaned over to listen. 'Was it ticking?' I thought. He casually booted the suitcase with his size-ten combat boot, and it slammed over on its side with a thud.

'Fuckin' hell!' The café guy was off, with me following right behind him. I walked all the way around the station to enter from the other side and get on the next Heathrow Express, waiting for a bang the whole time.

The last time I'd heard a bomb go off, a really big bomb, was in 2001 when I was working in Nigeria. Anyone who has worked in Nigeria will know the expression '419', after section 4-1-9 of the Nigerian Penal Code, which relates to fraudulent schemes. I drove in through the office gates, it was a lovely sunny day. The vultures were all lined up on the office roof—the base was only a stone's throw away from the Port Harcourt slaughter market—and were looking down at the office staff and workshop technicians, who were all standing outside in the carpark.

The first thing that jumped into my head was, 'Fuck, they've all gone on strike.' But no, I was told we had been robbed and that the security men had been found out the back, gagged, tied up and smelling of shit.

On entering the office we found the place trashed, tables and chairs upside-down, and the safe opened with the aid of a sledgehammer. There were expatriate passports all over the floor. The safe we had purchased locally some months earlier, and by the looks of things it wasn't the first time it had been broken into; lumps of car filler had broken off its shell. We didn't keep the petty cash in the safe—it came back to the staff house each night—so the thieves ended up stealing passports, the fax/copier machine and the company communication equipment, VHS and VHF radios.

Later in the morning the local CID arrived on the crime scene. They told us they needed a photographer, the loan of a car and driver, some money for food and drink or, as they say, 'minerals', before they could start their investigation and apprehend the criminals. The officers then took advantage of the car for the rest of the week, without coming up with a thing, so we decided to drop the case and get back to as normal a working life as you can expect in Nigeria.

One of the passports that got lifted was mine, which meant I had to go to Lagos to get a new one. I stayed in a staff house on a very busy, very dirty road. It had huge solid iron shutters on the windows and another for the front door, and every night the house was closed up like the dark ages, both to keep the locals out and us in. I was only going to be there for a few days so I didn't mind too much. My first night was spent chatting to the other two guys who were also temporarily staying there. One of the guys worked for a well testing company. He was in Lagos because his warehouse had been broken into and the thieves had made off with some very powerful high explosives which we use inside special tools that are sent down the well to fracture a formation.

The second night I was halfway through dinner, eating at the coffee table in front of the TV, when the whole house and everything in it, including me, appeared to go up a few feet then crash back down again. The TV fell forwards onto its screen and blew up, glasses and plates smashed on the kitchen floor, the windows flexed and shattered in their frames. The other two guys in the house came sprinting out of their rooms, one in his jocks, the other in coveralls. We all went for the front door. The lights had gone out, so we fumbled at the bolts on the iron door, then finally it swung open and we spilled out onto the street. Car alarms shrieked in the distance, I could hear children screaming. At the end of the street where an apartment building had stood a few minutes earlier, there was a big pile of rubble. A giant cloud of concrete dust roared down the street, swallowing up everything. We ran back inside and bolted the door.

'How much of that shit did you lose?' I asked the well tester.

'That much,' he replied.

The following morning the sirens were still wailing up and down the street as I got in the car to go and get my passport. By the time I had done that and jumped on the next flight to Port Harcourt, the story was on the news. It was the well tester's high explosive that went off the night before. Some would-be bank robbers had stolen it, improvised a device using all of it, put it in a car and parked the car in the basement carpark of the apartment building; it was supposed to be a distraction from the real drama, the bank directly across the street, which they had planned to knock off. Not realising how powerful the explosive was, and not doing a very good job of rigging it up, they all went bang in the car and vaporised at two thousand feet per second, as did the whole building.

Our base in Port Harcourt was a five hundred-square metre concrete compound, with various workshops and two single-storey office buildings, all surrounded by a high concrete wall festooned with razor wire and protected by armed guards on duty twenty-four hours a day. Every morning we would run the gauntlet of impoverished locals waiting for our car to arrive at the main gates. It took a few minutes for the guards to unlatch the lock and swing open the doors, and in that time the car would be surrounded with requests for a few *naira*, Nigerian currency, and sick babies would be pressed against the window. Begging with babies is, unfortunately, something I've seen many times in many parts of the world, and occasionally the infant is quite obviously dead. If there was time before the guards came out and pushed them all away, we would slip them a few bucks.

During a particularly hot still day, I was working on some equipment in the middle of the yard. We had so much equipment in the base at that time there was no more space left to work in the shade. So, using the forklift, I dumped everything in the open and set up an umbrella. Two guys were giving me a hand, and we passed the morning chatting about the usual stuff as we worked. Then around lunchtime I noticed they were shooting glances over to the far wall near the corner. There was nothing over there at all. 'What's going on?' I asked.

'Target practice' was the response. Then I saw a man's head and shoulders appear at the top of the wall; it was fifteen feet high so he must have been propped up on something. I looked closer. It was the handicapped guy I had seen begging at the front gates.

The two blokes I was working with suddenly produced slingshots from their pockets and began firing rocks with money wrapped around them at the poor guy's head. I stood there horrified. 'What the fuck?' A rock bounced off the guy's head, but he didn't go down.

'Do you want a shot?' One of the blokes, the bigger one, offered me his homemade slingshot.

'No, I don't want a fucking shot! Stop it.' They ignored me and went back to their fun. The rocks were small bits of dried cement wrapped with money, and occasionally they disintegrated against the wall in a puff of dust and paper. But every shot that went high would have sent the beggars on the other side into a frenzy. This had obviously been going on for some time, and all the people on the other side of the wall had ganged up on the handicapped guy and made him the target.

'Cut it out.' I tried to stop them.

'Make us,' said the big one without looking at me.

'You guys are fucked!' I wasn't getting into a brawl, but I had to stop them somehow without creating a problem. Then the handicapped guy dropped down and that was it. In the five minutes he was up there, they had fired off perhaps twenty dollars in small bills; the poor sod they were shooting at only got hit once and that, it seemed, was an acceptable reason for his pals to grab him and shove him into the line of fire.

The next day when I arrived at the workshop gates I saw him off in the background; he was sitting with his back against the compound wall and drooling while the others banged at the car windows. Later that morning I thought of a way to stop him from getting hurt, but still allow the money to keep coming in. I told one of the other guys about it.

'What are you going to do?' he asked me.

'Do you know who Ned Kelly is?' I said.

'Ned who?' He had just come from South Africa on his first job overseas so I didn't bother explaining it to him.

'Google it,' I said and went off to the paint shack to get a bucket. Once I found the right bucket, I washed it and cut out a little slot so that when Ned had the bucket on his head he would be able to see what was going on. Then I tied two rubber straps to the brackets that held the handle. I went out through the gates with the bucket and found Ned still sitting there in the same spot. The others weren't quite sure how to react to me and just watched. I stuck the bucket over Ned's head and ran the straps under his arms. He may have been sitting there in his own shit and drool but he knew that with his new bucket he wasn't going to lose an eye in today's session.

I went back to work on our tools in the yard with the two sadistic maniacs. Bang on lunchtime they pulled out their slingshots and loaded up. Ned appeared, his head rag-dolling from side to side, and they lost it, unloading all their cash at Ned and missing altogether. Ned was a hit. It went on for the rest of the week, and by then Ned was cashed up. On the following Monday morning he was sporting a new shirt, his bucket under his arm as he waved and howled at me through the window of the staff car, spraying the entire vehicle in spittle. Another week went by and Ned was in new shoes, and he'd painted his bucket and stuck bottle caps all over it. He was ecstatic.

Christmas that year was good for the crew, and everyone got a bonus. We got a cheque and the local guys got what they wanted; not cash, that was too simple. They wanted to be given a gallon of cooking oil, a twenty-five-kilo bag of basmati rice and a live chicken on Christmas Eve. So the company made sure it was the right type of oil the majority would expect, that the bag of rice did weigh twenty-five kilos and not nineteen, and especially, that the chickens were all alive and kicking; no Nigerian wants a dead chicken, with no electricity at home for a fridge. Christmas was good for Ned too. He got a new stainless-steel bucket with foam and rubber lining to reduce noise, and a slingshot so that if by chance his hand–eye coordination somehow returned, at least he could shoot back.

A good tip for anyone going to work in Nigeria is that you will be asked on more than one occasion, 'What have you got for me?'

The answer is, 'My blessing on you and your family.'

Trust me—it works every time.

3·PHILIPPINES 2000

PHILIPPINES

IMMIGRATION

ARRIVAL

Date

Flight

Status

Stay

折らないで下さい。

カード②は出国時に入国審査官へ提出

* Please type or print.

* Do not fold.

* CARD ② is to be submitted to the

at the time of your departure from

DEPARTURE

JUN 24 2000

Status

26 JUIL 83

United Kingdom of Great Britain and

Passport

PHILIPPINE IMMIGRATION

Visa Pursuant to Memorandum

Order No. Permitted to stay

up to

05 08 04

Александровск

САХАЛИН

Россия

Surname/Nom

Code of Issuing/Code

CARTER GBR

16 09 04 5<

18 09 0

Given names/Prénoms (2)

Chief Dep & Ext Section

Nationality/Nationalité (3)

19

O.R. No.

Date of birth/Date de naissance (4)

Sex/Sexe (6)

M

Place of birth/Lieu de naissance (7)

Date of issue/Date de délivrance (8)

PHILIPPINES

IMMIGRATION

ARRIVAL

JUL 2000

11 THIS LITTLE PIGGY

Home in Sydney again after our honeymoon, Clare was back at work and I was sorting out my visa for my next job in Russia. This time the campaign was supposed to be an improvement on last year's shambles. I sat in my office remembering how miserable I got out there. But most of all I remember how hungry I was by the time we got from the rig to the hotel, a day later. I ate leftover bread rolls off room service trolleys in the hotel corridors on my way to go out and eat with the boys. That's hungry. Money before you eat when you've been offshore on a rig that serves dog food has no value at all.

Last year after a massive three-month Russian stint we gathered in some nice restaurant. As usual it was Erwin's choice—I think he instinctively knows where to go. We had each purchased one of those bargain-bin business shirt and nasty rayon tie combo packs, and we arranged ourselves around an expansive table adorned with pressed tablecloths and silverware as if we were the rulers of our own special empire. It was worlds away from shuffling along with plastic trays in our hands. Ambu clapped and read out the name of the company that printed the menus for the restaurant. We ordered an aperitif and read the menu with Ambu. It felt like we were about to have the greatest meal of our entire lives.

Before, during and after dinner we decided to drink, along with wine, a great deal of gin and tonic. Last time it was vodka, before that single malt, before that tequila and so on, from one end of the bar to the other in more than a dozen fine restaurants around the world. As usual everyone degenerated into 'male-violent' lunacy, everyone except Erwin; he always maintains control of himself and thereby us, which explains why we haven't been kicked out of more than a dozen fine restaurants around the world.

'Would this gin and tonic help me to avoid malaria?' I asked Erwin.

'No.' He was studying the label on the back of the bottle.

'What if I had another one?'

Erwin looked over at me. 'The gin and tonic, Pauli, was created as a way for Englishmen in tropical colonies to get loaded in the middle of the day while at the same time ingesting their daily dose of quinine, used to ward off malaria, right?'

'Right.' Excellent, I thought, he's off, he's going to tell me all about gin.

'Modern tonic water still contains quinine, though as a flavouring rather than a medicine. To answer the question of how many modern G&Ts would need to be consumed to deliver a preventative dose of quinine? Sixty-seven litres.' He was well and truly off. How does he know that? Why does he know that?

Ambu was loving it. 'I like gin,' he beamed.

'Let's have a martini, Ambu,' I suggested and grabbed the cocktail list.

Ambu started reading out the names on the list. 'Pink Slapper,' he said as his stumpy finger moved across the letters.

'Slipper,' Erwin corrected.

I found the gin-based cocktails, nudged Ambu and, doing my best Sean Connery voice, said, 'Why don't you slip out of those wet clothes and into a dry martini, young Ambu?'

He gave me a blank look. The waiter came over and we ordered three martinis, shaken not stirred.

'James Bond ruined the martini,' Erwin was off again. 'A martini is made with gin, and shaking gin muddles its flavours and clouds its appearance. Ambu, you could be a Bond villain.' Erwin was laughing. 'But you'd need a shaved cat and a collarless shirt.'

Ambu looked blank again.

'So where does gin come from, mate?' I asked Erwin, who was back to the label on the bottle.

'Oh, gin has a dark past, more daunting and evil than any Bond villain. It's steeped in black history, it fuelled a billion drunks through Britain's lowest moments. The Dutch started the whole thing in the lowlands of Holland. One Dr Franciscus de la Boë in the university town of Leiden created a juniper- and spice-flavoured medicinal spirit that he promoted as a diuretic. The new creation spread fast. It was the late sixteenth century. The Dutch christened it "jenever", the linguistic root of the English word "gin". Initially it was sold in chemists to treat stomach complaints, gallstones and—are you listening, Ambu?—gout.'

'I have gout,' Ambu replied, sipping slowly on his martini.

Much later, we were full, after the wine was gone and we squeezed in a cheese platter and dessert, and a glass of brandy, and one of those little mints, and coffee with its little cookie. My belt had gone back two notches and there was a cigarette butt in Ambu's mash potatoes. Erwin and John were talking Don out of cutting off his other little toe with a cigar cutter. Don had his shoe and sock off, and was convinced he'd 'stop walking funny' if he removed and no doubt cremated it. Then they moved on to motorcycle header pipes. I was telling the others to share the cigar trolley, someone threw the cigar cutter at me, and that was when John made the international sign for 'the bill'.

Getting the waiter's attention can involve everything from making eye contact to discharging a firearm in some parts of the world. But then you do a pantomime of writing something on your palm while mouthing the words 'THE BILL' at your waiter, a sign recognised universally. When it does arrive it's passed around and everyone scratches their head for ten minutes, and inevitably it's shoved in front of whoever's turn it is to pay. The argument is that some countries are more expensive than others. But that's the system, it works out in the end; you could get nailed with a thousand-dollar bill in Japan and one month later its two hundred bucks in Thailand.

This year's Russian campaign surprised me. I was overjoyed to see that improvements had been made, and while the job was going to take three months again, this time we would get changed out with a fresh crew after six weeks. We had a great room on the rig, the shower had hot water, the toilet flushed, the food was edible, but best of all the people in charge were back again. Colin and Ann Smith are a remarkable couple.

They are the only husband-and-wife 'company man' team I've come across (these are people who work on equal time rotation—month on, month off—with the 'back to back' person in the team doing your job while you're on your month off). I try to imagine having Clare as my 'back to back' on the rig and I can't. They are superb people to work for, and they have been working like that for years.

About halfway through my six weeks I was in Colin's office, having a chat, when he told me about a land rig he and Ann had worked on years ago in Colombia. The rig was in the Cupiagua basin, deep in the jungle. They were frequently attacked by local rebels, who would take a shot at the rig every few days and on a weekly basis try to blow something up. The location was completely surrounded by a high wire fence and security personnel were on patrol twenty-four hours a day.

Not too far from the rig was the tool pusher's cabin with the company man's cabin next door. The company man and the tool pusher basically ran the whole operation between them, making them highly desirable targets. The portacabins were very basic, just thin plastic over a metal sub-frame. Inside, the layout was just as simple—a desk, small closet and a metal-framed bed, with a foam mattress on top. The tool pusher hated the bed, and every time he crew-changed back to the rig he moaned about his bed to Ann and Colin. So with the tool pusher's birthday not too far away, Ann and Colin decided to get the onsite chippy to make him a fantastic new bed. The carpenter did a great job, making a huge frame with two massive drawers underneath, and Ann and Colin got him a big sprung mattress. The real motivation for the new bed, however, was for the drawers in its frame as the tool pusher was really keen on dirty magazines, and Ann was fed up with walking into his portacabin after he had been in there for a month and finding his cock mags all over the place. So a month later the tool pusher came back out to the rig, walked into his portacabin and discovered he had a huge new bed with two drawers full of porn—what more could a tool pusher want?

A few days later the rebels strong-armed one of the local guys who worked on the rig to plant a bomb in the tool pusher's cabin. They had the device in a box and the timer was set to go off in the middle of the night. The tool pusher went to bed at the end of his shift as usual, and in the early hours of the morning the bomb went off. The blast shook the whole camp, and the tool pusher's cabin disintegrated, but he survived. His massive collection of dirty magazines saved his life, they absorbed the shockwave and, along with the new bed and mattress, he was propelled through the roof and into the night sky.

The whole job went very well, even the Azerbaijanis avoided their usual brawling, and Mother Nature left us alone as well. My hitch was soon over. Erwin asked if Clare and I would like to go to his place in Perth for Christmas. Erwin's is exactly the kind of home you want to wake up in on Christmas morning. His wife, Lucy, produces meals that make you wish you could eat your bodyweight, and his kids, all four of them, are great fun. He has a living room not unlike Captain Kirk's bridge on the starship *Enterprise*: one big comfy chair and a plasma TV that fills the entire wall. There are motorcycles, dogs, cats, rabbits and a huge backyard with a giant trampoline that gives me head injuries every time I get on it. In all, I look forward to a Christmas at Erwin's place.

Most of all, I love the bikes. Erwin has the same fascination with motorcycles as I do. Whenever we get the chance and we're not both on a rig somewhere, we have track days. Erwin rides a Jap 500 single in a Norton wide-line featherbed frame. I, on the other hand, ride a Kawasaki 650 Twin; it's a modern bike designed to look like a classic, but he still rounds me up. The bike I'm riding now is my second after I dropped my first bike twice. Riding a motorcycle is total joy, right up to the point when your overconfidence causes your first big 'Get Off'. My first 'Get Off' was just plain stupid.

After a long flight home from West Africa, suffering jet lag and everything else that goes along with modern economy air travel, I arrived in Sydney in the early hours of a Friday morning. It was summer, I was happy beyond words to be home and away from the diabolical shit that you have to deal with in West Africa. I'd spent the last few weeks on the rig constantly thinking about riding my bike when I got home. And here I was at last. I hit the ground running and went straight to the garage. I didn't bother showering, or perhaps waiting a day so I could get some sleep and allow my body to adjust to being home. No, I was going for a ride. With the battery reconnected and a full tank of fuel, I checked the tyres, threw on a jacket and bolted down the street. I was free, completely free, no-one was going to give me any shit or ask for a bribe or shoot at me. I'm in Sydney, where the roads are made of tar not dust, where road rage is just verbal abuse not a loaded gun, where people will go to extraordinary lengths to avoid a fight.

The hours passed, and halfway through my second tank of fuel I stopped in Bondi for lunch. The girl waiting tables outside was nice, we flirted a bit as I paid my bill, she asked about the bike and we chatted about it for a while. It was turning into a typical hot crowded Bondi day; the street was full of people, all the cafés were packed. My bike was parked directly opposite the table I was sitting at. The waitress walked me over to the kerb and I pulled on my helmet and sunglasses. 'Ride safely,' she said and winked at me.

'Ciao.' I threw my weight down on the kick-start and the Staintune exhaust blew a wonderful note across the sidewalk, turning everyone's head in my direction. The street was clear, I gave her my best casual wave and she waved back with a white napkin.

Twisting the throttle wide open and dropping the clutch, I felt my back wheel spin off the kerb, the bike slid into the open street and I roared off—a whole two metres. Then the disk brake lock I had put on when I parked bit into the front fork, instantly stopping the front wheel and sending me on a long, unimaginably embarrassing flight over the handlebars, where I executed an interesting mid-air turn and landed on my back in the middle of the street. My bike flipped over, also landing on its back next to me. The entire street stood up and clapped.

Needless to say, I never again forgot about the disk lock.

My first motorcycle experience was at my mate Andy's house. All the other neighbourhood kids hated Andy because after we had all banded together to build the best billycart in history the year before, Andy crashed it into a parked car at the end of the steepest street in town. He sustained head injuries and lacerations to most of his body, he smashed his sister's horse-riding helmet and, of course, we all kicked the shit out of him for crashing the cart, so Andy was shunned from all things.

But Andy had a postie bike. The great Australian 110cc postie bike, a fine machine, delivered the nation's mail for decades. Built by Honda, it is in fact one of the bestselling motorcycles in the country; it's bulletproof. And Andy also had a big shed with a huge old couch in it, a fridge and, best of all, a ping-pong table. That was enough; I was fifteen and I would have been friends with Pol Pot if he had a ping-pong table.

Andy and I would pour his mum's olive oil over the bike's back wheel and 'smoke it up' in his driveway. Eventually, I talked my parents into letting me have one, and after months of chores and odd jobs I had enough for a bike. Andy and I would ride around the streets, blowing up people's letterboxes with firecrackers, ride around the local golf course at night and generally make bastards of ourselves. At that age it was the most fun I was going to have with my pants on.

Then I met Debbie, and that changed everything; there was no more time for Andy, I was far too concerned with the intricacies of one-handed bra release. One weekend my parents went away and left me in charge. So the first thing I did was talk Debbie into coming over. After a lot of fooling around I finally had her naked and bent over on our new couch, her head unceremoniously buried under the armrest. I had successfully negotiated a condom over my penis after several failed attempts that included actually looking at the instruction booklet. This was going to be fun. My mother walked through the front door on the first stroke. Our eyes met, my jaw dropped and I fell forward in slow motion, my hands slipping off the armrest and sending my spotty teenage face into the scalding hot iron pipe protruding from the top of the pot-belly stove. My mother was not happy, Debbie was not happy, and I had a huge round blister in the centre of my forehead and no chance of getting any girls naked on the couch in the near future, so I was not happy. The only person who thought it was great was John; he just winked at me and pissed himself laughing.

Ten years later, after getting off a rig, I was taking a break in Perth and decided to look up Andy. He had gone into his family's construction business and had done very well. Andy had stayed in touch with all the boys who grew up in the neighbourhood and we planned a big reunion. So I found myself standing in the pub where we had all had our first legal drink ten years earlier; it had changed hands a few times over the years, and its current guise was kind of upmarket and boring. We gathered in the middle of happy hour near the garden bar at the rear of the building. There was Andy, myself, Bob, Dave and Michael. Bob had turned into a degenerate gambling junky and had gained two hundred pounds; Dave was making surfboards for a living and looked happy; Mike was married, had two kids and ran a pharmacy in a shopping mall, he'd aged twenty years.

The pub was crowded. Dave fought his way to the front and started passing drinks back to us, but it was taking forever. I didn't mind as my alcohol tolerance was shot after a month on the rig, and my nephew could have drunk me under the table. But Andy was pissed off. 'I'll be back in ten,' he said and walked off.

'What's he up to?' I asked Mike.

'Oh, he's going to one of the other bars in here—there's five, but they're probably all as crowded as this.' He nodded towards the garden bar then added, 'Or he's going to shit somewhere public.' Mike finished off his beer and shook his head.

'He what?!'

Mike leaned in, fiddled with his shirt tails and gave me a strained look as if it hurt to tell me. 'Andy has a shit fetish.'

'Oh fuck off, I've known him since we were kids,' I protested.

'Mate, you haven't spent any time around Andy since you were in your teens. He's got a problem. He's a great bloke, he's done really well for himself, he's just into poo,' Bob said, backing Mike up.

Dave walked up with five beers. 'Good to see you, Pauli. Cheers, mate.'

We all had a drink, then Mike said to Dave, who was holding a spare beer, 'Andy just walked off five minutes ago.'

'Oh fuck, he's not that pissed already is he?' Dave asked.

'What?' I looked at Dave blankly.

'Mate, last time we went out, he gets blind and takes a dump in some guy's car. Yeah, he reckons the bloke stiffed him on a business deal last year. We saw him park his car on Loftus Street, and Andy jumps on the roof, pulls his pants down and drops one through the sunroof.'

I burst out laughing, but wondered if the boys were having a lend of me.

'He's sick, and he's got issues with women,' Mike chipped in.

Andy came back and the boys went quiet. 'I can't tell which one of you four looks most like my dick,' he said.

I looked him in the eye. 'So the boys have been telling me all about your shit fetish, Andy.'

'Oh bullshit, it's not a fetish. Here, hold this.' He handed me a shot glass.

'What's this?' I asked.

'One shot of Baileys,' he answered.

'You went over to another bar to get this?' I put it down on the table.

'No, I went to get one of these.' Andy pulled a vending machine condom from his pocket, opened it up, took the glass of Baileys and poured it into the condom. All four of us just stood there looking at Andy, who looked back at us like we'd just asked him to kick a kitten into a woodchipper. 'That fuckin' idiot behind the bar is useless, so I'm going to fuck with her,' he said, and marched over to the packed garden bar. We slowly followed, but no-one said anything.

Andy, looking perfectly respectable in his designer suit and silk tie, quietly waited in the corner, then casually tossed the condom onto the back shelf behind the bar. The whole bar was black marble, and within seconds someone saw it and freaked. Soon after, the entire crowd at the bar had stopped yelling 'two vodka Red Bulls' and instead had become transfixed on the condom.

The poor girl tending the bar didn't know what to do. She was young, probably in college, and I noticed she was flustered with the demanding punters. You have to lip-read orders and mix multiple drinks fast to work in a place like this, and she wasn't coping with bottom-shelf drinks. She called the manager, he turned up with the big set of keys hanging off his belt, took one look at the condom and said 'Clean it up,' before walking off. She went over to the corner and came back with one of those little pivoting dustbins on a pole that you sweep up cigarette butts with, and a small broom. After five minutes she had the condom grasped in the middle, using the dustbin and broom like giant chopsticks, then she dropped it, spilling some of the Baileys on the counter. 'AAAAAH,' the crowd jeered.

That was when Andy launched himself across the bar and grabbed the condom. He grinned at the crowd, stretched it out, tipped it up and poured the contents into his mouth. One girl threw up on the spot. I turned and walked straight out, telling the guys where I was going in case they wanted to join me. I didn't look back, the place went nuts, bouncers sprinted past me towards the soon-to-be-battered Andy as I walked out.

An hour or so later we had all regrouped in a nightclub in a different part of town. I was standing at the bar with Dave, looking at an untouched Andy. He had apparently bought his way out of trouble, and was now sitting in a booth with four women around him, ordering drinks, the centre of attention and loving it.

'He's turned into a twat,' I said to Dave.

'Yeah, well, he can afford to, I s'pose.' Dave was as easy-going as ever.

We stayed there for a while, milling around and enjoying ourselves, then Andy was there next to me. 'C'mon, we're leaving,' he looked stressed.

'Why?' I asked.

'No time to explain.' He pulled on my jacket.

'Hey, fuck that, Andy, I like this place,' I said. 'What happened to your ladies?'

He didn't answer, he just left.

Dave and I stood there watching the girls in the booth. One of them opened her handbag and took out a packet of cigarettes, then paused and looked into her bag. Her girlfriend leaned in and peered into the bag as well. Then from somewhere inside she pulled out a neatly wrapped paper towel and out rolled a six-inch turd. It hit the glass-topped table in front of them and continued rolling all the way to the middle where it sat among their drinks. Four high-pitched almost perfect Hitchcock screams completely blanked out the music, and kicked off a stampede that emptied the dance floor and threw half the place into a panic. And all because Andy's completely depraved, sick little mind had decided it was a good idea to hide a turd in a handbag.

The final straw for me came right at the end of the night. We were all very drunk and trying to get a taxi, a five-seater taxi, at four in the morning in the middle of town; we had about as much chance of finding one as catching a lift home in the Pope mobile. Then Bob had an idea. 'Dave, you're the smallest, hide behind that wall,' he said and pointed at a tree, but we knew what he meant. 'I'll get the next taxi that comes round the corner, he will stop 'cos . . .' Bob stopped to stare at the pavement, swallow and focus. 'There's only four people and not five and he'll stop, you'll see.' He slapped his hands on his big belly and smiled the way you do after you've had so many beers you've lost count at twenty and you've completely forgotten what you're talking about.

There was a pause as we all grappled to understand Bob's idea. 'What? So everyone's in the taxi except Dave, he's hiding behind that wall,' Mike said. 'Not that I care, Bob, look I'll hide behind the wall, I'm supposed to take the kids to the beach today after church. It's Sunday morning now.' He was leaning against a bus stop and realising he was very late.

'No no no no, sorry, when the taxi pulls up, I'll open the door and Dave'll dive in and lay on the floor, then we all get in 'n the guy won't see Dave, you see,' Bob explained.

'Aw fuck off, fat boy. You lay on the floor of a filthy taxi and we'll all stand on your head,' Dave protested. He had beer hidden in all his pockets and threw one at Bob. The can hit Bob square in the forehead. Nothing, no reaction, he just rubbed his head then took off after it.

'I'll do it,' said Andy.

'Fine, great idea, I'll get the taxi.' I stepped into the street looking for the light on the roof, and right on cue a taxi pulled up. Bob was honking about the beer, not the fact that it had been thrown at him, but because it exploded in his face when he opened it. The confused Bob distracted the driver, Andy slipped in and lay quietly in the foot-well and the rest of us piled in.

Bob was in the front seat. 'Fremantle, please,' he said and grinned at the driver, beer dripping down his drunk face, and we drove off. All three of us who were sitting in the back exchanged the same look, then Andy farted. Mike kicked him in the ribs and that was it.

The driver's hand shot up to the mirror and angled it down to see Andy's head rearing up to confront Mike. He slammed on the brakes, ripped on the handbrake and went bananas. In seconds he was out of the taxi, the door was open and Andy was getting dragged out by his hair. The taxi driver was big, Italian and obviously at the end of a bad shift. Andy came up swinging and missed, and Mike and I got in the middle of it and tried to calm the cabbie down. Bob was waving his arms in the air, and Dave can speak some Italian and joined in, but while we all collectively talked the driver down, Andy had gotten into the driver's seat, closed all the doors and locked them. The driver was the only one facing the car, and he suddenly stopped gesticulating and his face went red. We all turned to look. Andy was unscrewing the black buttons at the tops of the doors, the ones you lock the doors with, and eating them. He swallowed all four, then clicked the column shift into gear and just drove off.

The five of us stood there for a moment, then we scattered in four different directions, leaving the poor cabbie standing there; he didn't know who to chase, and this was before mobile phones or any of that shit. I felt awful as I ran up a side street. Andy had issues, and I was hoping he didn't shit in that taxi.

That was more than ten years ago, and I haven't seen Andy or any of the others since. Though I did hear through the grapevine that Bob had his stomach stapled, Mike is divorced, Dave is gay, and Andy is still Andy.

PASSPORT TAB
Name PAUL CARTER
IMMIGRATION AUSTRALIA
PERMITTED TO ENTER AND REMAIN
FOR RESIDENCE
ON - 9 AUG 1985
AUSTRALIA
Perth Airport 10
07 JUN 2001
THỊ THỰC NHẬP XUẤT CẢNH
USED
HOÀNG SƠN THO

12 THE LAST STAND

'Do you realise what the human body goes through when you have sex? Your pupils dilate, arteries constrict, your core temperature rises, your heart rate and blood pressure skyrocket. Your respiration becomes rapid and shallow, your brain fires bursts of electric impulses from nowhere to nowhere and secretions from every gland. Muscles tense and spasm with enough force to move three times your bodyweight.

'So why waste money by joining a gym?' the doctor said, beaming back at me. 'And the best part is, you can make a baby.'

Good advice indeed.

'You're in good shape, Paul, just stop with the damn cigarettes.' This guy is good, he's been giving oilfield hands their work medicals for years, and his demeanour is a result of that. He's seen it all, guys walking into his office with everything from missing digits and broken backs to galloping jungle crotch rot. He's about fifty, Australian and looks a bit like a hippy crossed with a King Charles spaniel.

I was there because I'd just come off a rig that served a turkey at lunch the previous day that was so undercooked a skilled veterinarian could have saved it. I had casually asked if the doctor thought it was a good idea if I joined a gym, and he was basically telling me to spend my time at home in bed with my wife—nice one.

'Sorry, honey, doctor's orders.' I could see it now. Most guys after months offshore tend to leave their loving partners feeling like a seafront village after the Vikings have been through it.

The crew and I would be back the next day for our work medicals, and I didn't want to be throwing up while I was there. The doctor gave me some pills and I went back to my hotel to spend the rest of that day vomiting.

The following morning I was sitting in his waiting room again, this time with the crew. I hate waiting rooms; after all, it says 'Waiting Room' on the door, and there's no chance of not waiting, you have to just sit and wait. It's like standing in a long queue at the post office, it's infuriating and you end up thinking rotten things about the person standing in front of you. He's got dandruff, the fuckin' loser, or why hasn't she moved up in the queue, there's a huge gap, are you blind? The waiting room is even more annoying when you're there for a work medical—you don't feel sick so you really don't want to be there. And these days, it's not just touch your toes and read the board with one hand over your eye; it's full body scans, X-rays, blood, pee and poo in cups, climb this, run on that. It takes days.

I looked at the magazines on the coffee table in front of me. No matter how hard you resist, you will end up reading a three-month-old copy of *Woman's Day*, but that only lasts so long. I looked at the boys. Ambu's got gout, so I was hoping I would go in before him 'cos he'll take ages. Don pulled out the pages from copies of *National Geographic* and sniffed them 'because they smell like childhood', apparently, then he folded them into Japanese origami animals that were actually very good. Jake drew penises on everyone in *Newsweek* with a texta pen. Erwin has infinite patience, he just goes to his happy place or something, but then a Harley went past. A Harley Davidson exhaust note is like a dog whistle to Erwin: his ears twitch, his head cocks to one side, and he's up and over at the blinds to look.

My new guy was there cracking his knuckles. I hate that. John's a young American, hardworking, full of beans, keen to learn, and still copping endless shit for rubbing one out during a training course while wearing a heart monitor. He went in first, but came back out after only ten minutes or so. He sat down quietly and started thumbing through a magazine. We all wondered why he came out so fast. 'What's up, mate?' I asked.

But before he could answer, the doctor stuck his head round the door and said, 'Hey you, young guy, stop jacking off into your footy sox. You've got tinea on your bell end.' There was a long pause, and with that he called in Ambu. As soon as the door clicked shut we started laughing.

'Still thinking about that fuckin' nurse, John?' said Don looking up from his origami folding.

'Yeah well, at least I don't get shit stuck up my ass,' yelled John before he stomped off to the coffee machine.

Don furrowed his brow. 'That's an inherent contradiction,' he said and went back to his folding.

'You need to think about a plausible reason for your toes, Don.' Erwin looked serious.

'What, you mean just being a fuckin' sociopath isn't good enough?' John was getting past it.

'Screw the nut, mate,' I said. I could see this turning into a brawl. Don closed the magazine, his face turned to stone. He got up and walked over to John, who puffed out his chest and changed his stance. His voice also goes up half a dozen octaves when he's scared, whereas Don's goes down. This makes Don sound like he should be doing voice-overs on beer commercials.

Don's jaw was set and he was wearing a smile, but behind it was John's first real beating and the young guy knew it. You see, John's a nice bloke, and that's where his problems start. Nice blokes with nice wives and happy children don't go toe to toe in a waiting room, but Don does.

'Fuck off,' said John in a high-pitched squeak, sounding about as frightening as David Beckham. John was backed into the corner, then Don held out his hand and gave him a beautiful origami bird.

'I'll give it some thought,' said Don and burst out laughing.

Almost an hour later Ambu finally came out, armed with lots of paper so he could go down the hall and give blood, and pee in one cup and poo in another. In the past, after receiving instructions to bring back a 'stool' sample, Ambu has gone off and returned with furniture, ice-cream, even cigarettes. The cups they give you for urine and faeces are the same size and dimensions; however, the main difference between them is that the one marked for number twos has a tiny shovel attached to the lid. So even if you had not yet mastered the English language, you should understand the purpose for putting the little shovel in the lid, thereby distinguishing the vessel's intended contents. This time Ambu got it right and he returned some time later, smiling, casually walking past us holding his cup that had an entire foot-long turd jutting out the top.

Two days went by, spent mostly in the Singapore workshop pretending to work, then we got the okay to go on our next job, in sunny Bangladesh.

If my career was a house, with Japan being the lounge room, then Bangladesh is the remains which stand in that muddy patch of the backyard.

The flight was average, only remarkable because Don didn't stab anyone, or make obscene hand gestures at old people, or ask complete strangers to pull his finger, or drink soy sauce, or push foreign objects up his nose and wander into first class, or stare at small children until they got paranoid, or push John's face into his lunch, or strike up a conversation with a pretty girl in one of five languages only to start faking a twitch, or sniff hair, or smoke in the toilet—I could go on for days. We landed in Chittagong, and we gathered around the luggage carousel to wait for our offshore bags to trundle by. An hour later they appeared, and we filtered through customs and into the arrival hall.

Usually we have an agent or representative there to meet us, someone who has all the local info. They would help organise transport to and from a hotel, and to the heliport, for example, or bail Don out of the local lock-up in time for him to make it to the job, or pay off the local heavies after he put someone through a window, that kind of thing. But here we had nothing organised, so we ended up pairing off and climbing into three equally diabolical-looking, three-wheeler tuktuk things. My first car, a Holden Torana, was much like a two-door V8-powered strip club; it could kill half the Amazon every time you floored it. My current car is also a Holden, only a new one; it trundles along on a shot glass of fuel and Chanel No.5 comes out the tailpipe. What we really needed right now was a 'Paris to Dakar' Land Rover, especially when getting to the hotel turned out to be one giant game of chicken.

In Bangladesh, the crap coming from the exhaust of our transport was black but actually cleaner than the air that went in. The air was so filthy that when the six of us walked into the hotel lobby, we looked like we'd just arrived for the Al Jolson convention.

Our chopper out to the rig was going to be early the next morning so we all shuffled off to our rooms to relax and get some sleep. The hotel looked like a derelict building would if you wallpapered it and put gyprock over all the holes. I kicked the door shut and walked across the room to dump my thirty-kilo offshore bag on the desk. On the floor there was a nasty-looking purple oval rug, and as soon as my right foot hit the middle, it disappeared into the floor. My bag combined with my bodyweight was too much for the old floorboards, so there I was, looking at my left leg jutting straight out from under me. I was surprised that I could hear Don swearing. I scrambled to get up, luckily the rug had protected my right leg from the splintered wood. I pulled the rug back up, got down on all fours and peered through the hole into the room below me. Don was sitting on a chair, smoking a cigar and looking up at me. We laughed for a full five minutes.

At the time, Bangladesh was experiencing some problems of its own. In Dakar the people were rioting and this had spread to the outlying areas, so to be on the safe side we all stayed indoors that night. Not that an upset local here is a big problem; if we were in Korea, I'd be worried. We were in Seoul once when the locals decided to have a riot, and no-one goes off like the Koreans. They all go at it like their hair is on fire, I especially like the matching headbands. As we were about to leave, Don went missing. He'd gone out drinking the night before the riot started and never came back to the hotel. So eventually we packed up his gear—I had his passport and offshore pass—paid his bill and left for the harbour to jump on a supply vessel bound for the rig. At the last minute Don arrived at the jetty in the back of a packed ute, with his new friends chanting and punching the air. Don didn't have any of his original clothing on, he was wearing a headband and sporting a split lip, and didn't even know what the riot was about.

The Bangladeshi rig was a joke. It sat in the middle of a swamp, an old Russian jack-up that was more rust than anything else.

The company man was a perfect caricature of a company man. The brim of his massive plastic ten-gallon cowboy safety hard-hat came round the corner, followed several minutes later by a beer gut and a classic old-school oilfield attitude. They're thinning out now, these older guys; one by one they're retiring. They came up in the days when the rigs were hard as fuck, and they were screamed at, abused and tormented by tool pushers and drillers who would appear quite mad on a drill floor now. The ones who survived were the hardest, and it's these characters who you see now and again running a drilling operation. You can tell if they're old-school simply by the way they walk, and the way they will run off (fire) someone for no reason, but I like them because of what they say. And at least you know exactly where you stand.

'How's it going?' I nodded towards the drill floor, smiled and stuck out my hand.

The company man spat a wad of chewing tobacco on the floor, crushed my hand until my toes hurt and grinned. 'There's more oil in ma fuckin' hair. Check your tools.' He turned and sauntered off, packing a new wad of chew into his black bottom lip.

Two weeks later I'd lost nine kilos, apparently the average for anyone who ate in the galley. The rig had tried to kill us from the outside too, the main staircase simply falling off one afternoon, just after we had all used it. Then the next day a five-inch gooseneck fitting protruding from the floor exploded across the main deck with 2800 psi behind it. That's a bit like putting a landmine in the local park.

The whole operation was a mess, and after all the drilling was done, we didn't find a thing.

Things come full circle eventually; time catches up with all of us in one way or another. I'm happy, in all of the four dimensions. For me the rigs are an endless source of adventure and torture at the same time.

I'm sitting in a small crew room next to a land rig in the Japanese mountains as I write this. I've been up for more than thirty hours, the coffee is shit and it's starting to wear off. The blizzard outside the door has turned the rig white, and I can just make out the drill floor through the horizontal snow. Ambu and Don are asleep on the floor near the heater; I'll wake them up soon so we can help the guys on tower to rig down. We're all getting older—half of the crew are hitting their mid-fifties—and pretty soon it will be like running pipe with the cast from *Cocoon*. We'll shuffle in walking frames towards the rig and hope no-one puts their back out.

You get used to the oil patch, and you become used to white noise, to pain, to wearing huge industrial orange earplugs to bed every night because the big guy in the bunk above you snores like my mate Steve's French Mastiff being hot-waxed, and come to think of it you get used to the guy who looks and acts like Steve's dog. Now I'm talking about a gigantic drooling beast that lays all over the furniture, only gets up to eat and wets itself when you come home. Imagine a grown man that can do an 'excitement wee' after hearing the words 'chopper home'.

By tomorrow Don will be trying to drag Erwin and me out of a Tokyo motorcycle shop and into a bar, Ambu will be eating something that looks like it was rolled onto his plate by a dung beetle, and Jake will be getting new ink via a bamboo needle and the steady hand of a master tattoo artist apparently favoured by the Japanese mafia. The rest of us will fall back happy in each other's company.

Erwin just picked up the last stand of pipe to run in the hole. It's 2 a.m., Tuesday I think. The last stand, the last job for this year. I wonder what Clare is doing. She'll be happy to know I'll make it home for Christmas. I pick up the payphone on the wall in front of me and dial home, the sound of Clare's voice transporting me to a better place. For anyone who does what we do for a living, you don't need me to tell you how hard it is to maintain a normal relationship. Drilling rigs have been looming over my subconscious like a fat oilfield zeppelin ever since we decided to start a family.

'There's a letter here for you,' Clare says. I ask her to open it. 'It's good news.' She is smiling, I can hear it in her voice. 'You know that oilfield desk job you always wanted to have a go at? Well, I'm looking at it.' I'm ecstatic, I've been waiting for that letter for more than a year. My phonecard is about to run out. 'One more thing, honey,' she says, 'I'm pregnant.' The line beeps and cuts off.

Erwin comes through the door, stamping the snow off his feet and waking up the sleeping beauties. The wind snatches the door and slams it shut behind him, leaving the cabin looking like a pillow just exploded. No-one notices the blank look on my face. Erwin pulls off his hard-hat, and that smile spreads across his face through the melting snow around his upturned collar. He cracks his neck and rubs the back of his right knee—it gets sore in the cold after one too many bike crashes and thirty years on the rigs. 'Just another glorious day in the oilfield,' he says and grins.

15 FEB 2006

PERMITTED TO REMAIN IN SINGAPORE FOR THIRTY DAYS FOR SOCIAL VISIT ONLY FROM DATE SHOWN ABOVE.

IMMIGRATION AUSTRALIA
19 AUG 2005
DEPARTED
AUSTRALIA
SYDNEY AIRPORT 3480

Royal Nepalese Embassy
Bangkok, Thailand

Type/Type
Code of Issuing State/Code de l'État émetteur

Passport

20 MAR 1989

Nationality/Nationalité

Date of birth/Date de naissance (4)

TOURIST

VISITOR VISA

Sex/Sexe (5)

Place of birth/Lieu de naissance (6)

16 JUN 1989

SINGLE

Date of issue/Date de délivrance (7)

AT A PORT OF ENTRY

Date of expiry/Date d'expiration (9)

BANGKOK

17 MAR 1989

UNITED KINGDOM OF GREAT BRITAIN AND NORTHERN IRELAND

ROYAUME-UNI

Passport No.

Name of bearer
Nom du titulaire

Accompanied by spouse
Accompagné de son épouse

and by
et de

National status
Nationalité

BRITISH CITIZEN

No. of passport
No. du passeport

Attention is drawn to the notes at the back

Authority/Autorité

AUS

Holder's signature/Signature du titulaire

CARTER<<PAUL<ALEX

RE-ENTRY VISA R 0258861

FEDERAL REPUBLIC OF NIGERIA · RÉPUBLIQUE FÉDÉRALE DU NIGERIA

SEEN AT THE IMMIGRATION HEADQUARTERS

Name of Bearer

19 AUG 2005

PERMITTED TO REMAIN IN SINGAPORE FOR THIRTY DAYS FOR SOCIAL VISIT ONLY FROM DATE SHOWN ABOVE.

SINGAPORE

13 THE WHOLE OIL THING

I wanted to round everything out, I wanted to have a conclusion, an answer. I set out to make something as smooth as the prime minister's bedsheets, but somehow I ended up with an oily rag.

Time is money in oil. Every minute, every hour, every single day, year after year, the BPD (barrels per day) must keep pumping life into the system, a system that since the end of World War II has grown into a monster with an appetite that redefines insatiable. Feeding the monster via our global umbilical network has given us ease of progression into a new disposable push-button life, but mother's milk is going to give us all umbilical whiplash that could take it all away forever.

Perhaps I have a jilted, somewhat negative view of human nature. After all, we're products of our environment. I'm free, I live in a free market economy, I have the right to choose everything from soap to government, I can make or lose money according to my individual goals or fuck-ups, and if I don't like any of that I'm free to piss off and live somewhere else.

The huge amounts of money we spend fighting wars for oil and building ever-smarter smart bombs could perhaps be spent on deepwater exploration. Instead we feed our lust for selective destruction; now there are bombs which discreetly enter buildings through the letterbox and vaporise anyone whose eyebrows are too close together. It's a lot like the space race in the 1960s, when the sheer idea of getting to the moon was unbelievable, back when bombs just went bang and history judged the military not by what they aimed at but by what they hit. Why is this Earth-bound frontier so formidable, or own inner space overlooked?

This is an ocean planet. It's so big and completely mystifying. Take the Pacific Ocean: it covers half the globe, and you can jump on a plane and fly non-stop for twelve hours and not see any land. How much oil lies out there? All of the offshore drilling so far has occurred around the edges if you like. The future is a race to meet demand by pushing the boundaries of deepwater exploration. And the open sea is a formidable opponent. Off the coast of West Africa at the moment we are drilling into the seabed without damaging the life that exists there, other than the hole itself in six thousand feet of water, and down to twenty thousand feet of real estate, but we are far from reaching the uncharted depths. Sixty per cent of the planet is covered in water more than a mile deep, and it's largely unknown; more people have been into space than have explored the deep sea.

To drill for new oil out there, within the most powerful force in nature, will take engineering like never before. There could be trillions of barrels out there, enough for us to stop killing one another long enough to find an alternative to fossil fuels that works. Out in the open sea, a rig is vulnerable; forget the sheer depth, the surface alone can slap a rig around with a savagery that's difficult to describe in print. I've been offshore in bad weather and felt real fear pulling at my 'what if' strings; anyone who has looked over the deck into a dark, heaving, white-capped, freezing liquid hell will know what I'm talking about.

Mother Nature is to be feared and respected like no other, but perhaps we have finally reached a point where we can beat her down. We are neither savage nor wise, it's our half-measures that are the worst of it for Mother Nature. Overharvesting, deforestation, habitat destruction, war and pollution will cause, possibly within a hundred years, the biggest mass extinction event since the end of the dinosaurs sixty-five million years ago. In the beginning Mother Nature reached our soil and made it hers. After only a million years or so of doing nothing, we have come leaps and bounds, especially in the last hundred years, a millisecond for her. Old greed and corruption dies hard, makes men blind, drives them mad enough to devour her heart and turn her into a memory walled up in a zoo. There is more life on our planet right now than ever before, more than one and a half million different life forms exist. These are remarkable times; this new century will mark either the greatest era of human discovery or the end of 50 per cent of our planet's biodiversity.

But that's just my opinion. Any questions you may have, please direct them to: god@theblindingwhitelight.com.

ACKNOWLEDGEMENTS

A great many individuals have my thanks this second time around: Clare, my wife and my universe; Erwin Hergzeg, always in my corner, and his amazing family have my eternal friendship; the inspirational Sally and Simon Dominguez, and their single malt; Claire Atkins, a remarkable woman; Greg Waters, who underestimates the importance that his contributions make; Klaas van der Plas; Dave Sadler, a man who can really ride a motorcycle; Ross Luck; Steve Tunley; Vince and Sheman Moritti; Miranda Culley; Johnathan and Angela Catana; the De La Vega family; Geof Pacecca; Allan and Terri Cole; Steve, Phynea and Anastasia Papal—legends all. My family Al, Liz, France, Elinor, Johannes, Callum, Rory, Alex, Mathew, James, Daniel, Carrie, Cathy, Phillip, Fingal and Tamsi (happy trails).

The lovely and completely brilliant team at Allen & Unwin: Jo Paul, your critiques turn what would otherwise be one long fart joke into a book; Lou

Johnson; Catherine Milne; Alexandra Nahlous; Julia Lee—you all perform the literary equivalent of teaching a monkey how to perform brain surgery every time you take a manuscript off my hands, and you make it look easy. Thank you for going in to bat for me so many times.

All the Singapore crew, especially Drew, Les, Hiram, Myles, Adam, Ramat, JJ, Tahir, Fauzi, Joey, Bidin (who nearly cut his head off last year—glad you're still with us, mate) and Razac, rest in peace brother.

Ambu (take that belt off), John, Don, Jake (back in the big house), Avas, Barry Reilly, Dave 'The Seal Basher' Nordli, Vodka Bob, Fat Tony, Robin, Eddie, Ronny, Smithy, Colin Henderson, Ann Smith, Sick Boy, Well Head Willy, Donald Millar, Damian Forte, Pilso, Sam Leon, Wongy, John Logan, Chris Glennon, Cameron Westholt, Tony Lacey, Capt Tom Naude, Sqd Ldr Chris Boucousis, the manager of the 'Romper-Room'.

And Officer Young, sorry about the mess, and thanks for being gentle with me.

Special thanks to that Afghan guy near Gardez, by the side of the road somewhere between Camp 87 and Kabul on 21 April 2006, who decided not to shoot me—much appreciated.

All of you, lying in your bunks on a rig, we are multiplied and defused throughout the world, be safe, godspeed.

Readers' reviews and emails to Paul Carter for *Don't Tell Mum I Work on the Rigs, She Thinks I'm a Piano Player in a Whorehouse*

Hi, Paul, that was one of the best books I've ever read, and I've read friggin heaps. Just wanted to tell you that was the closest I've ever come to pissing my pants laughing whilst reading a book. Please write more.

Al

Have you ever picked up a book and not been able to put it down? I was literally in tears last night I was laughing so hard. The funniest book I have ever read, by miles. Although I am paying for it now after sitting up till 3am this morning to finish it. Highly recommended.

Ron

Great book, never have I experienced belly laugh with a book. My wife thought I was nuts. Hurry up and write another!!

Craig, New Zealand

Paul, just read your book on a flight across to the US on business. One of the funniest books I've read in a long time. I think the cabin crew were not far from sectioning me when I read the bits about Joe the monkey. Good luck and keep up the good work.

Andy

Thanks for a great read. It's the first book I've ever bought and I couldn't put it down. I read it in two days. It has opened my eyes to the world. I'm gonna have to get off my arse and do some travelling. Thanks mate ya truly bloody Australian!

Wesley

My husband is a sat diver (we have been together for coming up 13 years now) and I have just finished reading your book—I couldn't put it down until I finished it. I have never laughed so fucking much in my life.

You described so much of what I have heard of. I wanted to thank you for writing your experiences down as I was able to see them clearly and in turn see my husband's experiences more clearly—and shudder whilst giggling about them!

Our 15-year-old son has just grabbed it and is already laughing and coming in and pointing out places that he has heard about and telling me that 'Dad has done stuff like that too'. When our 10-year-old grows up more he will read it too and will be able to learn more about Dad's other life.

I learnt today that your book is doing the rounds of the vessel that my husband is on in the Gulf of Mexico and all the boys out there are enjoying the read—even the ones that don't read are reading it!

You are truly a fucking champion and thank you for bringing a smile to a rig pig's wife!

Jen

Hi Paul,

I'm an Aussie living in London and a mate's just returned home from Sydney with your book. I'm down to the last 10 pages and I don't want it to end. I'm not normally much of a reader but luckily yours fell within my 'under 200 pages' limit and scored double bonus points for 'big words AND pictures' :) Above all it's very very funny shit.

Would love to buy you a beer . . . in fact there's a small fan club of mates now that agree we'd just sit ya down, get ya drunk and let YOU do the talking.

Congratulations on the book you've done a fantastic job. I can't wait for the next one.

Sam

Hello there, just finished 'dont tell mum', fuckin brilliant book, couldn't put it down. Keep 'em coming Paul, highly entertaining when you're sitting in your cabin.

Dan

Dear Paul,

Just read your book non-stop in a three-hour sitting. As the partner of an Aberdeen offshore worker and having lived in the oil community for most of my life I just wanted to say how utterly marvellous your book is and how much I enjoyed it. I laughed like a drain from start to finish. Many thanks for a hugely entertaining evening!!!

Fiona

A mate leant me your book, read it twice in 2 days when I was in Bali in March. A lot of people stared at me and gave me a wide berth because I was laughing so hard I had tears running down my face . . . can't wait for your next book.

Anonymous

Hi Paul, I picked up your book in the A&R bookstore yesterday and wanted to let you know that I'm loving it. Wonderful storyteller. You have me captivated. I'll be buying my Dad a copy for Father's Day. He's about to head off to WA to drive dump trucks at an iron ore mine. My Uncle works on the oil rigs. Maori guy . . . called Tom Ormond . . . ⋆laughs⋆ . . . well you never know! All the best for the second book.

BTW, what bike is that on the back cover?

Rosie

From a current resident of Bumfuk Nowhere, to a former resident: I've just finished your book and wanted to pass on how inspirational it was. The fact that it had me laughing like a village idiot on the train and in the office was only a bonus.

My brother works on rigs and will soon start working for a large spillage recovery company. If his experiences ever come close to rivalling yours, then I will be deeply and dangerously jealous.

Thanks for the laughs and if you can offer any tips as to where I might acquire a smoking monkey buddy, I'd be forever grateful.

Paul

ALSO BY PAUL CARTER

DON'T TELL MUM I WORK ON THE RIGS
She Thinks I'm a Piano Player in a Whorehouse

"This is Carter's romper-stomper tour of the world's oil rigs. It's a highly enjoyable tale."
The Glasgow Herald

A take-no-prisoners approach to life has seen Paul Carter heading to some of the world's most remote, wild and dangerous places as a contractor in the oil business. Amazingly, he's survived (so far) to tell these stories from the edge of civilization.

He's been shot at, hijacked and held hostage; almost died of dysentery in Asia and toothache in Russia; watched a Texan lose his mind in an Asian jungle; lost a lot of money backing a scorpion against a mouse in a fight to the death; and been served cocktails by an orang-utan on an ocean freighter. And that's just his day job.

Taking postings in some of the world's wildest and most remote regions, not to mention some of the roughest rigs on the planet, Paul has worked, got into trouble and been given serious talkings to in locations as far-flung as the Middle East, Borneo and Tunisia, as exotic as Sumatra, Vietnam and Thailand, and as flat-out dangerous as Columbia, Nigeria and Russia, with some of the maddest, baddest and strangest people you could ever hope not to meet.

IT'S ALL GREEK TO ME!
A Tale of a Mad Dog and an Englishman, Ruins, Retsina – and Real Greeks
John Mole

"Travel writing at its best. Mole's descriptions of the people and places he encounters do for Greece what Peter Mayle did for France in A Year in Provence and Frances Mayes for Italy in Under the Tuscan Sun."
www.greece.com

"A little whitewashed house with a blue door and blue shutters on an unspoilt island in a picturesque village next to the beach with a taverna round the corner…" This was the dream of the Mole family in search of a piece of Greek paradise.

But a beautiful view and a persuasive local prompted the impulsive purchase of a tumbledown ruin on a hillside with no water, no electricity, no roof, no floor, no doors, no windows and twenty years of goat dung…

In a charming saga of sun, sea, sand – and cement, John Mole tells of the back-breaking but joyous labours of fixing up his own Arcadia and introduces a warm, generous and garrulous cast of characters who helped (and occasionally hindered) his progress.

John Mole has had a varied international career, from banking in the USA and Athens to jacket potato restaurants in Russia. He is also a well-known author of comic novels and the perennial bestseller *Mind Your Manners*.

UK £7.99, US $14.00 Paperback 978 1 85788 375 6
352pp 198x129mm
www.nicholasbrealey.com

MISADVENTURE IN THE MIDDLE EAST
Travels as Tramp, Artist and Spy
Henry Hemming

"A once-in-a-lifetime journey, full of youthful ebullience and idealism, but self-aware too, and brave."
Colin Thubron, author of Shadow of the Silk Road and The Lost Heart of Asia

A beautifully written tale of a hapless artist, a truck called Yasmine and an extraordinary journey, creating a portrait of the post-9/11 Middle East that transports the reader into the human heart of the region and beyond the stereotypes.

Making art his passport, Henry Hemming's year-long travels take him from the drug-fuelled ski slopes of Iran via the region's souks, mosques, palaces, army barracks, secret beaches, police cells, nightclubs, torture chambers, brothels and artists' studios all the way to Baghdad and a Fourth of July party with GIs in one of Saddam's former palaces. From being accused of being an Islamic extremist to the Turkish army forcing him to make portraits of their girlfriends, from dancing in a dervish hideaway to being interrogated by the secret police as a British spy, *Misadventure in the Middle East* reveals an alternative Middle East that flies beneath the radar of the nightly news bulletins.

Henry Hemming is a British artist with a first-class degree in history from Newcastle University. He now works in a cramped East London studio and you can see examples of his work at www.henryhemming.com.

UK £10.99, US $19.95 Paperback 978 1 85788 395 4
304pp 214x135mm
www.nicholasbrealey.com

THUMBS UP AUSTRALIA
Hitchhiking the Outback
Tom Parry

"Tom Parry took on one of the marathons of hitchhiking – the round Australia route – and he has written a colourful and amusing account of the journey."
John McCarthy, Excess Baggage, Radio 4

Hitching lifts with the desert's dodgiest drivers and taking breaks in the roughest roadhouses, this is Tom Parry's witty, warts-and-all tale of hitchhiking 8,000 miles across – and around – the Australian outback with his thumb, his backpack and his French girlfriend Katia.

As the couple hitch their way around the near-empty highways they encounter as wide a cross-section of Aussie society as you could ever hope to meet. In cattle stations, Aboriginal communities, remote waterholes, caravan parks, hippy communes and roadhouses, they see a country that remains as extraordinary today as it was for the first nineteenth-century settlers.

Thumbs Up Australia features some of the country's most idiosyncratic characters, from the grizzled Aboriginal elder with his tales of dreamtime, to an amphetamine-swallowing roadtrain driver.

After trying to establish himself as a drummer in a rock band, **Tom Parry** is now a journalist with *The Daily Mirror* and has written travel articles for magazines such as *Traveller* and *Wanderlust*.

UK £9.99, US $16.00 Paperback 978 1 85788 390 9
288pp 214x135mm
www.nicholasbrealey.com